A King Production presents…

MEN OF
The **Bitch** *Series*
AND THE WOMEN WHO
Love Them

A Novel

JOY DEJA KING

Cover concept by Joy Deja King
Editor: Jacqueline Ruiz tinx518@aol.com

Library of Congress Cataloging-in-Publication Data; A King Production
Men Of The Bitch Series And The Women Who Love Them/by Joy Deja King
For complete Library of Congress Copyright info visit;

www.joydejaking.com
Twitter @joydejaking

A King Production
P.O. Box 912, Collierville, TN 38027

A King Production and the above portrayal logo are trademarks of A King Production LLC

This Book is Dedicated To My:

Family, Readers, and Supporters.
I LOVE you guys so much. Please believe that!!

—Joy Deja King

"I Only Want To Love You Twice In My Lifetime.
That's Now And Forever..."

~A Woman In Love~

A KING PRODUCTION

MEN OF
The Bitch *Series*
AND THE WOMEN WHO
Love Them

JOY DEJA KING

Chapter One

Adrenaline Rush

Before Precious Cummings stole their hearts, there was another woman both Nico Carter and Supreme shared. But until this day, they never knew it. Her name was Vandresse Lawson and although she loved them both, she was only in love with herself and it cost her everything.

"Girl, that color is poppin'. I think I need to

get that too," Tanica said, eyeing her friend's nail polish as the Chinese lady was polishing them.

"You bet not! We ain't gon' be walking around here wit' the same color polish on," Vandresse huffed.

"Won't nobody be paying attention to that shit," Tanica said, sucking her teeth.

"Stop it!" Vandresse frowned up her face as if. "You know everybody around here pay attention to what I do. All these chicks dying to be just like me," she boasted, admiring how the plum polish made her honey-colored skin pop.

Tanica glanced over at her best friend and rolled her eyes. She loved Vandresse like a sister, but at the same time Tanica felt she was so full of shit. But there was no denying, in the streets of Harlem: Vandresse was the queen of this shit. She was always the real pretty girl in the neighborhood, but once she started fuckin' with that nigga Courtney, it was on. Nobody could tell her nothing, including her childhood friend Tanica.

"I'll take that pink color," Tanica told the lady doing her nails. She had no desire to beef with Vandresse over something as simple as polish.

"So are we going to the club tonight or what?" she asked ready to talk about having some fun.

"I can't." Vandresse sighed.

"Why not? We've been talking about hitting this club since we first heard they was reopening it weeks ago."

"I know, but I told Courtney we would hang out tonight."

"Ya always hang out. Can't you spend a little time with your best friend?"

"Maybe tomorrow. I mean look at this tennis bracelet he got me." Vandresse held up her arm and slowly twirled her wrist like she was waving in a beauty pageant. "These diamonds are stunning. If I have to spend some quality time wit' my man, give him some head, sex him real good so the gifts keep coming, you gotta understand that," Vandresse explained with no filter as if the nail salon wasn't full of people, but of course she didn't give a fuck.

"I get it. I just miss hanging out with you. Brittany is cool, but she's not as fun as you," Tanica hated to admit.

"Of course she isn't, but it's not her fault. I'm the turn up queen." Vandresse laughed.

"Yeah you are." Tanica joined in on the laugh.

"But on the real. I miss hanging out with you too even though we're roommates and attend hair school together. But we haven't just hung out and had some fun like we used to. I wish Courtney had a cute friend I could hook you up with."

"Me too. Because that one you hooked me up with last time was not the answer."

"I know, but I was hoping his money would help you excuse his face," Vandresse said shrugging.

"How you luck out and get a dude who's cute and got money," Tanica stated shaking her head. "I can't believe out of all the friends Courtney got ain't none of them good looking."

"That's not true. One of his friends is a real cutie, but he just a low level worker. But he can afford to take you out to eat and buy you some sneakers... stuff like that. At least we would be able to do some double dating. If you want me to hook you up just say the word."

"Let me think about it. I don't know if I wanna sit around watching yo' man shower you wit' diamonds, all while homeboy taking me to

Footlocker, so I can pick out a new pair of Nikes."

"You so crazy." Vandresse giggled before both girls burst out laughing while continuing to chat and make jokes while finishing up at the nail salon.

"I figured you would wanna chill tonight," Vandresse said looking in the passenger side mirror as she put on some more lip gloss. "I did say I was gonna treat you extra special tonight for icing out my wrist so lovely." She smiled, using the tip of her freshly manicured nail to tap the diamonds on her tennis bracelet.

"I didn't forget. I'ma hold you to that." Courtney winked, squeezing Vandresse's bare upper thigh. "But umm, I told my man Anton I would stop by for a second. He poppin' some bottles for his birthday. Nothing major. He keepin' low key. But we do a lot of business together and I promised I come through."

"I feel you." Vandresse smiled not really caring either way. She was already plotting on how she was going to suck his dick so good tonight so she could get a diamond ring to go with her bracelet.

"But when we leave here, it's back to the crib so you can take care of Daddy." Courtney nodded.

"You know I got you, baby." Vandresse licked her lips thinking how lucky she was to have a sexy nigga who could fuck and was getting money out in these streets.

When they walked into the Uptown lounge it was jammed pack. "I thought you said this was low key," Vandresse commented.

"A lot of niggas fuck wit' Anton so they all probably coming through to show love," Courtney replied as he headed straight to the back like he knew exactly where he was going. Vandresse was right by his side, happy that she decided to wear a sexy dress tonight since there was a gang of chicks in the spot. When it came to stuntin' on other bitches, Vandresse was super competitive. She always wanted to be number one or at the very least top three.

"My nigga, C!" A guy who Vandresse assumed was the birthday boy stood up showing Courtney love.

"Happy birthday, man!" Courtney grinned. "I see everybody came out to show love to my homie."

"Yeah, I wasn't expecting all these people, but hey it's my birthday! You and your lady sit down and have some champagne," Anton said, playing the perfect host.

Courtney took Vandresse's hand so they could sit down. "Baby, I'll be right back. I need to go to the restroom. Have a glass of bubbly waiting for me when I get back," she said kissing him on the cheek.

"Excuse me, where's the restroom?" Vandresse asked one of the cocktail waitresses. The lady pointed up the stairs so Vandresse headed in that direction.

When she got to the bathroom, Vandresse was relieved nobody was in there. She wanted to check to make sure one of her tracks hadn't came loose. Vandresse always kept a needle and some thread in her purse just in case. She examined her weave and to her relief it wasn't a loose track brushing against her ear, it was her leave out. Vandresse glanced at her reflection one last time and after feeling confident she had her shit together, she exited out right as a handful of chicks were coming in.

Right in the entry way of the bathroom there was a huge spotlight. When Vandresse came in, the upstairs was damn near empty, but when she came out, there were a ton of people and all eyes seemed to be fixated on her. *Thank goodness I made sure I was straight before I walked out*, Vandresse thought to herself. She was heading back down stairs when she felt a firm grasp on her arm.

"Why the fu..." before Vandresse had a chance to curse the man out, she locked eyes with a nigga so fine she changed her mind.

"I apologize for grabbing on you, but I couldn't let you get away. You are beautiful. What's your name?"

"Vandresse," she uttered. The man's intense stare had her feeling self-conscious for some reason. Like his eyes were piercing through her soul.

"My name is Nico. Nico Carter. Come sit

down with me so we can have a drink." He spoke with so much confidence that Vandresse found herself following behind the stranger like her man wasn't downstairs waiting for her.

"I'm sorry. I can't go with you," she finally said, snapping out of her trance.

"No need to apologize. Did I do or say something to offend you?" Nico questioned.

"Not at all. I'm actually here with my man. He's downstairs waiting for me."

"Oh, really," Nico said unmoved. "That might be a problem for you tonight, but it doesn't have to be tomorrow."

Vandresse gave Nico a quizzical look. "I'm not following you."

"You're not wearing a wedding ring so you not married. Are you willing to miss out on what might be the best thing that ever happened to you?"

"Wow, you're a little full of yourself."

"Only because I have every reason to be. Give me your phone number. I'm more of an action person than a talker."

Vandresse wanted to say no because she had a good thing going with Courtney, but she also knew it wasn't a sure thing. Like Nico said, he wasn't her husband and they were both young. Vandresse wasn't stupid. She was well aware Courtney was still out there doing him. Vandresse knew she was his main bitch, but not his only chick.

"Here," she said, writing her number on a napkin then handing it to Nico.

"You're smart and beautiful. I think we'll get along just fine."

"We shall see. But I gotta go."

"Cool, I'll call you tomorrow." Nico stood at the top of the stairs looking over the banister and watched Vandresse walk over to a small group of people. A young dude stood up and took her hand and he figured that must be her man. Nico knew he needed to leave that alone, but the same way he got an adrenaline rush from dealing drugs, chasing a beautiful woman that was technically unavailable gave Nico that same high.

Chapter Two

Illusion Of Bliss

Before T-Roc settled down and became a married man and father of two, he had an unrelenting obsession with movie star Tyler Blake. He believed the Hollywood starlet was destined to be his. But once Tyler fell in love with Andre Jackson that left the door wide open for industry gold digger turned glorified baby mama Chantal

Morgan to step in.

Andre chose to marry Tyler even after Chantal unleashed every trick in the book to get her baby daddy to make an honest woman out of her. Instead of collecting her child support check and disappearing into oblivion, Chantal came up with a master plan. This time it was full proof. She set her eyes on T-Roc and this time she did pull off the ultimate feat. Chantal Morgan went from hooker to housewife by getting the notorious womanizer to make her his wife. But Chantal should've been careful what she asked for because this was one marriage that was doomed from the start.

"Where are you going?" Chantal questioned slipping on her five-inch Jimmy Choo Belle Chain Fringe T-Strap sandal.

"Out. I have a business meeting. Where are you going?"

"Shari's in town. I'm meeting her for dinner and drinks. You should come with me."

"I told you, I have a business meeting," T-Roc said casually picking up his wallet from the nightstand.

"I love how easy it is for you to lie to me."

"Chantal, what are you talking about?" he questioned with irritation in his voice.

"I guess going to fuck Angela counts as a business meeting," Chantal shot back, putting on her diamond hoop earrings. "I saw her text message, T-Roc."

"The text message said nothing about fucking."

"I'm not stupid, but you know what, go right ahead and do whatever you like," Chantal said, reaching into her bathroom drawer and grabbing the small vial of coke. She took a quick hit before grabbing her purse.

"Don't you think you're getting a little too old to still be snorting coke."

"I guess I can ask you the same question regarding your whoring ways. How long are you going to keep fucking models, groupies, and industry whores? Or are you never too old for that. Just remember, while you're out there letting all these chicks suck your dick, two can play that game."

Before Chantal could hit the door, T-Roc had her back against the wall. "You're my wife and when you're out here in these streets you conduct yourself accordingly," T-Roc warned, gripping Chantal by her neck.

The thing was, Chantal wasn't afraid and when T-Roc stared deeply into his wife's eyes, he knew it. T-Roc had met his match with Chantal. He married a woman who was crazier than he was and he had no idea how to handle her.

"I know that I'm the wife of a well-known and respected music mogul. I would never do anything to disrespect you in public," Chantal mocked with a devious laugh. "Now I need to go. Shari is waiting for me and Angela is expecting you, so excuse me."

T-Roc released Chantal from his grasp and this feeling of dread came over him as she walked out their bedroom door. He had this love/hate relationship with his wife. They shared two children and after all these years of marriage the only reason he hadn't filed for divorce was because even with all the craziness, T-Roc was still very attracted to his wife. Chantal lacked many things, but beauty and sex appeal wasn't one of them. Plus, when she felt like it, she was insatiable in bed and knew exactly what to do to please T-Roc.

"Sorry, I'm late," Chantal said to her best friend Shari when she sat down. "Thank goodness you already ordered a bottle of champagne because I need a drink."

"Please, I would expect an apology if you were on time. I mean you're always late," Shari said laughing.

"True, but I'm trying to change my ways. I'm lying." Chantal giggled, pouring herself a glass of bubbly. "But it sounds good saying that," she said smirking. "Anywho, girl, I'm so happy you're here. I wish you would move to New York. I have no girlfriends here. Dare I say I'm ready to move back to LA?"

"When you lived in Beverly Hills you hated it too. You complained all you did was have play dates. You felt you had turned into a Hollywood suburban mom. If being both is even possible," Shari joked.

"I know, but at least it kept me busy. But now my kids are older and they have lives of their own. As long as they have cars to drive and unlimited access to credit cards they could care less about spending time with me." Chantal sighed. "I guess you could say I'm lonely."

"What about your husband. I can't imagine being married to T-Roc and being lonely because he's definitely a character."

"I said I was lonely. Never did I say I lacked entertainment," Chantal cracked. "Seriously, I do love T-Roc, but as I'm getting older his womanizing ways are starting to drive me crazy. I know before I used to act like those things didn't matter. All I cared about was the money and prestige. But I want to feel beautiful again."

"Chantal, you are beautiful. My gosh have you looked at yourself in the mirror. You're wearing those jeans like you're still nineteen."

"Yeah, well I have plenty of time to stay in the gym to keep my body tight, but that's becoming more and more unfulfilling," Chantal admitted. "I'm not nineteen anymore. I can't just throw on a freakum dress, hit the club, and for the moment make all my problems go away. Wow, if I'd known this was how my life was going to turn out, I would've went to school and had a career or at the very least developed a hobby."

"Chantal, it's not too late. You're still young and you have access to plenty of money. Use some of it to start a business. Figure out what you love to do."

"You mean besides shopping. That and being great in bed are the only two things I've truly mastered. But no matter how good I please my husband sexually, it doesn't keep him from fuckin' around. It's almost to the point that I don't want to have sex with him at all. I mean what's the point of being my husband's personal sex slave if it still doesn't make him keep his dick in his pants."

"I didn't realize you were so miserable. You always seemed so happy when we would talk or when we would visit each other. You appeared to have the glamorous life you always wanted. I hate seeing you like this, Chantal," Shari said concerned for her best friend's mental state. Through all the drama Chantal had been through, from trying to run down Andre in her Mercedes on their wedding day after he left her at the altar, to faking a suicide attempt to keep him from marrying Tyler Blake, she always seemed in control. Plotting on her next scheme to get what she wanted. She even plotted on making T-Roc her husband which actually did work out for her. But now, Shari could see that something was different. Chantal seemed to be on the verge of spiraling out of control and Shari had no idea how to stop her best friend from ruining her life.

Chapter Three

Back In The Game

Before Genesis realized the love of his life, Talisa, wasn't dead, but after killing Chanel with his bare hands, and discovering Chanel the woman he considered a friend, lover, and future wife was a psychotic monster, there was someone else. Her name was Qiana. She was the woman that believed her love could save Genesis from himself.

"I'll bring the kids back Sunday night," Robert told his estranged wife while picking up their two small kids. "Call me if you need me," Robert said leaning forward to kiss his wife, but she turned her cheek.

"Have fun with your father. I'll see you guys on Sunday," Qiana waved to her son and daughter before closing the front door. She walked over to the couch in the living room, sat down and placed her legs on the ottoman. Qiana leaned her head back and pondered how after seven years of marriage, she was now separated from her husband and about to be a single mother. Qiana felt she had done everything right so it was hard for her to understand how it all went so wrong. But before she could dwell on it any further she looked at the clock and realized she needed to get dressed so she wouldn't be late for work.

When Qiana arrived at The Four Seasons, it was already busy. She worked at the check-in desk and barely had time to put her purse down before she was bombarded with current and incoming guests. When Qiana's friend, Rhonda, told her she could hook her up with the job at the plush hotel she jumped at the opportunity.

The pay was good, the hours were perfect since she had gone back to school to go take some classes, and sometimes the guests would give her great tips when she was able to make their stay a little more pleasant. On the downside, it was extremely busy so she was overworked, most of the hotel guests were complete assholes, and she never got off on time. But with her current predicament, Qiana was in no position to make waves so she did her job with a pleasant smile on her face.

"Good afternoon, how can I help you?" Qiana casually gave her standard greeting as she multi tasked not yet making eye contact with the guest. She was trying to wrap up a phone call, but the woman on the other end seemed determined to make a simple five second conversation into a fifty minute one. "I apologize, what can I do…" Qiana found herself stopping before completing her sentence when she laid eyes on the man standing in front of her. Feeling embarrassed, she quickly tried to play it off. "Sorry, I was still thinking about the conversation I just had with the lady on the phone. What can I do for you?" She beamed.

"My name is Genesis Taylor. I wanted to check into my room," he said handing the woman his driver's license and credit card without her even asking. He already knew the drill.

"Thank you, Mr. Taylor. I'll get you checked in." Qiana smiled nervously. She wondered if the man could tell how in awe she was of him. He had the most perfectly chiseled face she had ever seen, with these dark, deep set eyes that hypnotized you without even trying.

"Take your time. If you don't mind me saying, you're stunning. I don't know too many women that could pull off that hairstyle," he said observing her close cut cropped jet black hair. "It truly compliments your beautiful face."

"If you're trying to win me over so I'll upgrade you, it's not necessary. You're already staying in a suite," Qiana said trying to contain how hard she was blushing.

"I'm only speaking the truth. You're an extremely gorgeous woman."

Qiana's heart was racing. Working at the front desk of an upscale hotel, she came in contact with tons of men, but none of them ever had this effect on her. "Thank you," she finally managed to say. "Well, Mr. Taylor, you're all checked in," she said handing him his room keys. "I see you'll be staying with us for a week. Are you here for business?"

"Yes, I am, but I'm hoping I can add some pleasure to that. I guess we'll see." Genesis gave a subtle smile and walked off towards the elevators.

"Omifuckin'goodness! Was that fine ass man flirting with you?! Why couldn't he have come to my counter," Margo came over to Qiana and said.

"I think he was, but I'm not sure. I don't wanna get too excited," Qiana said beaming.

"Girl, from what I overheard him saying to you, it sounded like that to me. Damn your lucky." Margo shook her head before heading back over to her counter.

Qiana thought about what her coworker said and she started getting butterflies in her stomach. She kept glancing over at the elevators hoping she would see the man walking back in her direction, but he never came. She then figured that the intimidatingly handsome man was just a flirt and had no interest in her. Qiana spent the duration of her time working her shift, full of disappointment.

Once Genesis dropped off his luggage in his hotel room, he wasted no time heading out to handle business. After being reunited with his sister Nichelle then having to kill Chanel, Genesis took a break from running his drug empire to spend some much needed quality time with his son and his sister. Although Genesis enjoyed being with his family, after a few months the streets began whispering in his ears and the voice became louder and louder until he could no longer resist them calling his name. Soon Genesis found himself becoming restless and he had to get back to work. Making lucrative drug deals was equivalent to running a Fortune 500 company to Genesis and he wanted back in.

That need led him to ATL. With Chanel no longer being in the mix, Genesis had to step up and lock down another connect. During their partnership, Chanel was the one that primarily handled securing potential suppliers, but Genesis would now be taking over and tonight he was having a meeting that he hoped would put him back on top of his game.

When Genesis arrived at the 3.5 acre estate in Buckhead's Tuxedo Park he was impressed. The exquisite English manor mansion was something of a masterpiece. The massive foyer opened up to a pair of arched staircases on both sides overlooking the two-story great room with a wall of windows with views of the infinity pool, outdoor living space and an expansive terrace. On the terrace level there were entertainment media, exercise, and spa rooms. The place came equipped with everything you needed to not leave the house if you didn't want to.

"Genesis, it's a pleasure to finally meet you," said Mateo, a slim, well-dressed Mexican man who greeted him with a firm handshake. The two men sat down in a room with complete privacy.

"The pleasure is mine. I know you're a very busy man so I appreciate you taking time out to meet with me."

"Quentin speaks very highly of you. He did a lot of business with my father. Of course I would take the time to meet with you. You tell me what you need and I'll make it happen."

"Just like that?" Genesis questioned with skepticism.

"You have two things working in your favor. One, you come with an excellent referral, and two; I recently had to cut off another gentleman I'd been doing business with. So I have a lot of product I need to move. You could be his replacement."

"If you don't mind me asking, why did the two of you stop doing business?"

"He was cheating me out of money. When it was brought to my attention, I didn't want to believe it. I had been doing business with him for many years and I thought he was a good man... I was wrong. Greed got the best of him. He made more money than he could ever spend because of me, but that still wasn't enough. I hope you won't be that sort of man, Genesis." Mateo's piercing green eyes seemed to be burning a hole in Genesis's head as if trying to read his mind.

"Mateo, I give you my word. If you supply me with drugs, I will do exemplary business with you. Never will I cheat you out of your money."

"Then you, Mr. Taylor, have a new supplier." Mateo stood up and reached out his hand and Genesis stood up more than happy to shake it.

"Let's make this money." Genesis smiled, thrilled to be back in the game.

Chapter Four

Is She Worth The Trouble

"Girl, we only have one hundred hours left until we finish this course. Then we can take our state exams and finally get our cosmetology license!" Vandresse exclaimed with excitement as she and Tanica were leaving their class.

"I know and I can't wait. Who knew you had to go through all this to do some hair. I swear I don't think know how that girl that work in that shop up the street from our apartment got a damn license," Tanica remarked.

"Fuck what they doing. I want my shit to be legit. Plus, Courtney promised he would open up a salon for me when I finished this class and passed my state exam," Vandresse boasted.

"Do you think he really will?" Tanica questioned.

"I hope he keep his word, but you know how niggas are. They pop all that shit until it's time to step up. Humph, I wouldn't be surprised if Courtney is secretly hoping I'll drop out and not even complete the course. But it ain't gonna happen. You know I've always loved to do hair. It's my passion," Vandresse beamed. "So Courtney will have to deal." Just then her cell started ringing. "I bet that's Courtney now.... hello."

"What you doing?"

"Who is this?" Vandresse questioned not recognizing the deep sexy voice.

"Nico. Did I catch you at a bad time?"

"No. I just wasn't expecting to hear from

you." *This is him!* Vandresse mouthed to Tanica as she enthusiastically pointed to her phone while keeping her cool as she spoke to Nico.

"Why would you have thought that?"

"I met you like a couple weeks ago. I figured you lost my number or decided not to use it."

"I told you I was gonna call. I wouldn't of said it if I didn't mean it. What you doing right now?"

"I'm actually just leaving cosmetology school," Vandresse told Nico.

"You do hair?"

"I sure do, but after I complete all my hours and get my license then I'll be legit."

"I feel you. That's what's up. So do you have time to go get a bite to eat? I wanna see you."

"I wanna see you too."

"Good. I'll come pick you up in an hour."

"Make it two."

"Cool. Text me your address. I'll see you soon."

"Omigosh! I can't believe he called!" Vandresse gushed when she got off the phone.

"That's the guy you told me you met at that lounge a couple weeks ago?"

"Yes! After all this time not hearing from him

I thought that was a bust."

"So you're going out with him tonight?" Tanica asked.

"Fuck yeah! Did I not tell you how fine his ass was?" Vandresse looked at her friend like she was crazy.

"What about Courtney?"

"What about him?" Vandresse frowned up her face. "It ain't like that nigga ain't fuckin' around. I would be stupid as hell if I put everything into him."

"I feel you, but the thing is that nigga takes care of you. You ain't putting no money in his pocket. You think he gonna let you fuck around on his dime."

"He ain't gotta let me 'cause Courtney ain't gonna find out. I'ma just have some fun with Nico, nothing serious so stop worrying. Now let's hurry up so I get home and get ready for my date tonight."

"I like your Benz," Vandresse said when she got into Nico's car. "This is reaaaaaal sexy," she beamed, stressing the word real.

"I like it too. I got it a week ago," he told her as he pulled off.

"It does still have that new car smell." She nodded glancing around and eyeing the spacious backseat. "I can't wait until I get my Benz. It's gonna be candy apple red with black leather interior," Vandresse said like she was picking it up from the dealership tomorrow.

"Nice... so when you gettin' this car?" he asked.

"I don't know, but hopefully soon. Maybe you'll buy it for me, or give me yours," she said sweetly as if it was a very plausible possibility.

Nico took his eyes off the street and glanced over at Vandresse who was sitting pretty and confident. He gave a slight chuckle before taking his attention off her and directing it back to the street.

"What's so funny?" Vandresse questioned. She figured he got a kick out of what she said.

"You're the type of woman who looks a man in his eyes and tells him what you want and how soon you expect to get it. I find that hilarious," Nico said continuing to laugh.

"Is there something wrong with that?"

"Not at all. As long as you know the more you ask for the more that is required of you."

"I can handle that as long as I get what I want," Vandresse remarked leaning back in the car seat. "Isn't that what life is all about... getting what you want or at least die trying." She giggled.

Nico rested his eyes on Vandresse when they came to a stoplight. Her dark brown and blonde ombre weave was laid perfectly. She wore just enough makeup to highlight her best features without going overboard. Her blouse and skirt accentuated her curvy figure to turn a man on, but not come across as an easy lay. Vandresse embodied the appearance of a very polished hood chick, the type of female that street niggas making a lot of money loved to wife up. But what

Nico liked most about Vandresse was her brash attitude. He found most pretty girls to be boring with no spunk. They were so busy trying to be cute, their personality was dead on arrival, but from the moment Vandresse got in his car, she was lit and he loved it.

When they arrived to the restaurant in Manhattan, Vandresse was impressed. The place was upscale and very classy. Although her boyfriend Courtney had plenty of money he would never think to take her to a place like this. He was hood rich with hood taste. Nico on the other hand was a tad bit older, more experienced. He had been places, seen things, and it showed with his selection for dinner.

"Wow, this night keeps getting better and better and we just started." Vandresse smiled. "You got class, Nico. I like that."

"I'm sure a girl like you is used to places like this," Nico said looking over the menu.

"Honestly, I'm not, but I can get used to it very quickly."

"So yo' man ain't wining and dining you?"

"Courtney treats me good, but he's not used to places like this. Hell, neither am I. He's nineteen and he hasn't been gettin' money that long. He tries though."

"I see. I can tell by that bracelet you have on. That had to cost him a nice chunk of change."

Vandresse gazed down at her wrist admiring the diamond bracelet that she never got tired of looking at. "Yeah, I was stoked when he surprised me with this."

"I know you said you're in hair school. Are you working?" Nico questioned trying to size up how serious her relationship was with this Courtney dude.

"No, I don't work. I'm just going to school."

"So how do you support yourself?"

"Courtney takes care of me," she replied not looking up from the menu.

"Let me ask you a question."

"Sure, what is it?" Vandresse answered still not making eye contact with Nico.

"Your man seems to be treating you right so why are you here with me?"

"Because you said that you might be the best thing that ever happened to me. I wasn't willing to take a chance and miss out on what sounded like a once in a lifetime opportunity. Can you blame a girl?" Vandresse peeked above the menu finally locking eyes with Nico.

"So you're an opportunist?"

"I guess that's one way you can describe a girl like me. I like the term ambitious better. I mean listen, I grew up in Harlem. I lived with my mother and grandmother. We didn't have no money, but yet I live in New York and all you see is money. What's wrong wit' me wanting a little slice of it? If a man wants to be the one to give it to me, why not."

"I get that. But you have a man that's taking care of you, but yet you're not loyal."

"But what if you can take care of me better. Plus, loyalty works both ways. Yeah, Courtney takes care of me, but he ain't loyal and like you were so quick to tell me, I ain't wearing no wedding ring," she said waving her finger. "I'm not married," she said smirking.

Nico eyed Vandresse with an intense stare. He began to wonder if this game he enjoyed playing with women should include the one sitting across from him. Nico was positive he would have a lot of fun with Vandresse, but he also got the sense she could also be a lot of trouble. Trouble he didn't need. Unfortunately, Nico Carter was a gambling man and the risks made the game all the more intriguing.

Breaking Point

Chapter Five

Before Lorenzo began a forbidden love affair with Precious, but after Dior—the woman he believed he was destined to spend the rest of his life with who was killed—he shared an intoxicating relationship with Chantal. A relationship that was so intense, it would change all of their lives forever.

Lorenzo's life had been on autopilot ever since the death of his beloved Dior. After beating his drug charges and getting out of jail, he focused on business, getting revenge on the people he felt were responsible for Dior's death, but other than that he was simply going through the motions. Falling in love was nowhere on his to-do list, but a man does have needs.

"I'll set up a meeting with the label and get this situation worked out. But you have to calm down," Lorenzo stressed to his artist, Phenomenon, over the phone while walking down East 57th Street heading toward the hotel he was staying at. "I'll call you later on once I get everything scheduled." As Lorenzo was wrapping up his phone call he noticed a chauffeur-driven big body Bentley pull up in front of the Christian Dior store. The driver got out and opened the door and at first all Lorenzo saw was a nude Gucci ankle wrap cage sandal with a gold buckle hit the sidewalk. Then his eyes zoomed in on the well-sculpted legs that came with the shoes. She was wearing a rose gold, silk belted dress that stopped mid-thigh. Her hair was up in a loose ponytail. Although her eyes were hidden behind designer sunglasses her beauty and sex appeal was undeniable. He hadn't been captivated by a woman's mere appearance since Dior, so Lorenzo had to know who she was.

When he entered the store at first he didn't see her. So Lorenzo walked towards the back of the store and there she was admiring a pair of shoes. His gut told him he should turn around and walk out the door, but his lust wouldn't allow it.

"I'm more than positive you can afford anything you want in this store, but I would love to buy those shoes for you. Just so I can see you in them," Lorenzo said, standing behind the woman.

"Excuse me?" When the woman turned around she was even more beautiful than Lorenzo thought and her perfume had a distinctive, exotic scent that made her even more alluring.

"You're gorgeous. Please, tell me your name."

"Chantal and thank you for the compliment."

"I'm sure you get them all the time."

"Actually, I don't," Chantal replied with sadness in her voice.

"I find that extremely hard to believe. You're damn near flawless."

"Wow, I don't know what to say." Chantal blushed. She then looked away nervously, hating she felt so grateful by the man's attention.

"I apologize if I'm making you feel uncomfortable."

"It's okay. Honestly, I'm flattered that a man as handsome as you is showering me with all these compliments."

"They're all true. Does that mean you'll let me buy those for you," he said nodding at the shoe Chantal was still holding.

"Oh these," she said as if she had forgotten they were even in her hand. "I truly appreciate the offer, but I'm married." Chantal held up her hand revealing an enormous rock.

"My apologies, I had no idea you were married, but I should've known a woman as beautiful as you would be taken. Based on the size of that ring your husband clearly loves you or he's just a show off." Lorenzo gave a slight smile that made Chantal laugh.

"I'm leaning towards my husband is a show off."

"That's too bad. A woman like you, it should be because of love." Lorenzo and Chantal spent a few seconds only speaking with their eyes. "I won't take up anymore of your time. Enjoy the rest of your day, Chantal," Lorenzo said turning to walk away.

"Wait!" Chantal put her hand on Lorenzo's arm. "Don't leave."

Less than an hour later, Lorenzo and Chantal were in his hotel room having passionate sex. For the first time in years, Chantal felt desired by a man. As Lorenzo's tongue kissed her hardened nipples and put her breasts in his mouth, she arched her back relishing in the pleasure of feeling alive again.

Chantal straddled Lorenzo as he grasped her ass pressing it deeper on top of his dick. It caused her to scream out from the pain as his massive tool filled up her insides. He began to rock slowly letting her juices drip down so her sugar walls could expand allowing her pain to turn to pleasure.

"Do you want me to stop," Lorenzo asked between strokes as Chantal continued to scream out in pain.

"No, please don't stop. You feel so good," she moaned as her body became in rhythm with his.

Chantal began biting down on Lorenzo's neck. "Fuck me harder," she groaned turning Lorenzo on even more. Each thrust became more intense as the two strangers had now become the best of lovers. They spent the duration of the day and night making love over and over again.

While his wife was having her back blown out at a hotel in Manhattan, T-Roc was engaged in his own torrid affair. He had three women he kept in rotation and today he was spending time with Harper at the penthouse he kept in Wall Street. Since Chantal knew nothing about the place, it allowed T-Roc the freedom to carry on with other women as if he was a bachelor.

"That was perfect," T-Roc exhaled with satisfaction after Harper got up off her knees from giving him a blowjob.

"So what are we having for dinner?" Harper questioned, putting on her bra and panties.

Although they didn't have actual sex, T-Roc liked his women to suck his dick butt naked.

"Babe, we can't order dinner tonight," T-Roc said putting on his pants.

"Why not?" Harper looked confused.

"Tracy, my assistant, is on her way over. I have some important business I need to handle."

"But you have to eat." Harper said sweetly, walking over to T-Roc and kissing his neck.

"Tracy is bringing my food. Here," T-Roc said pulling out a few hundred dollar bills from his wallet. "Go get yourself something eat. I'll call you next week."

"Fine." Harper took the money, but that didn't erase the disappointment from her face. Harper was well aware like all of T-Roc's other women that he was married with children, but that didn't stop any of them from believing if they played their cards right, they could knock Chantal out of her position and be the next Mrs.

"Don't make that face. You're a model. You don't need the frown lines." The tone of T-Roc's voice sounded as if he was concerned and only looking out for Harper's well being. He then stroked the side of her face as if to pacify her.

"Are you saying I'm getting frowns on my face?" Harper stood in front of the mirror and closely examined her skin becoming paranoid.

Instead of easing Harper's paranoia he headed downstairs when he heard the doorbell. "Tracy, you're right on time," he said letting his assistant in.

"I've been working for you long enough to know that you hate waiting," Tracy commented stepping inside. "I brought over the paperwork you said you needed, of course my laptop and your food. I'll go put it on a plate for you.

While Tracy was heading to the kitchen, Harper came strolling down the stairs still in her bra and panties. "Tabitha, did you bring me something to eat too?" Harper asked smugly standing in the middle of the staircase.

"The name is Tracy, but you already know that. And no, I didn't bring you anything to eat. I work for T-Roc not one of his many wh... or never mind." Tracy gave a sarcastic giggle and kept it moving leaving Harper mortified.

"T-Roc, did you hear her!? She was about to call me a whore."

"Harper, calm down. No, she wasn't. You

misunderstood her."

"No, I didn't. She was about to say one of your many whores. You need to fire her!" She was not only embarrassed, but also so angry her face was turning red.

"Baby, calm down." T-Roc was now coddling Harper.

"Why would she say something like that? Are you sleeping with her?"

"Of course not. Tracy has been a loyal employee for many years. I would never cross that line. She's the best assistant I've ever had. I wouldn't want to mess that up by adding sex to the mix."

"So you would have sex with her if she wasn't your assistant!" Harper yanked herself out of T-Roc's embrace. "That's what you're telling me right now. And what did she mean one of your whores? I thought I was the only one, T-Roc."

"You mean besides his wife?" Tracy taunted, walking back in the room with T-Roc's plate of food.

T-Roc shot Tracy an intense glare. She already knew what her boss was thinking and it was hilarious to her. Throughout her years of working for him, Tracy had a front row view of the many women who came in and out of his life. The end result was always the same.

"How dare you!" Harper screamed.

Tracy was about to light Harper's ass up, but T-Roc shot her another look and she knew that meant to shut the hell up. That's one of the reasons their relationship worked so well because Tracy knew exactly how far to push things and when to back down. Instead of continuing to stir the pot, she turned around and went back to the kitchen.

"How can you let her disrespect me like that? You need to fire her!" Harper yelled.

"That's enough," T-Roc said firmly. He lifted up Harper's chin. "It's not very becoming when you act like that."

"But I just love you so much."

"I know you do," T-Roc said before gently kissing Harper's lips. "Now go upstairs and get dressed so you can leave. It's time for me to get to work."

T-Roc let out a heavy sigh as he watched Harper go back upstairs as if she was defeated. Dealing with her made him work up an appetite. He went to the kitchen hoping his food was still hot.

"Here you go," Tracy said taking his food out the oven right on cue as she always was. She was a very smart woman and Tracy knew exactly what to do to keep those bonus checks coming in. T-Roc appreciated her handling his business, but the little things counted just as much. "Oh, and here's your drink."

"You're the best," he said needing a stiff drink.

"Looking a little stressed there, boss. I keep telling you, leave these young girls alone. They're not mentally equipped to handle a man like you."

"Stop being so hard on Harper. She's just a little sensitive, that's all."

"Please! You mean delusional. But it's your fault. You make all these women feel like if they just look and behave perfectly, they'll have a chance to be the one. But there is no the one for you, except for maybe Chantal."

"When did you become a fan of Chantal?" T-Roc questioned taking a bite of his food.

"I'm not. She's probably the worse of the bunch, but she's also the only one that knows how to deal with you," Tracy said rolling her eyes. "But everyone has their breaking point, T-Roc," she added.

"What is that supposed to mean?"

"Meaning that if you keep this up one of these women is going to snap. I've seen so many women walk in and out that front door. Each of them thinks they're more special than the next. Without warning you cut them off when you feel like they're becoming too clingy. But you make them that way."

"How do I do that? I'm always upfront and let them know that I'm married," T-Roc stated trying to defend himself.

"Yeah, you do, but you also make each of these women feel like they're special and give them a little inkling of hope. It also doesn't help that you're so generous with your money and gifts," she said frowning.

"That little bit of money I be spending ain't nothing," he scoffed.

"Not to you because you have so much of it, but to them it's everything. They also take it as another sign that you care about them."

"Listen, I like to spoil women. Just ask Chantal and Justina. I've given my wife and daughter so many gifts I've lost count. Hell, I'm always giving

you a bonus check even when a bonus isn't due."
T-Roc laughed. "My generosity is never gonna
change. That's who I am."

"But you're also a very cold man. I can tell
you that because I love you and not only are you
my boss, but we're also friends."

"I don't think I like where this conversation
is going, Tracy."

"I'm just warning you. A bunch of women
and a wife don't mix. How long do you think
Chantal is going to put up with all your cheating
before she starts cheating herself... hmm?"

"That will never happen. Chantal is my
wife and she loves the lifestyle too much to ever
jeopardize losing it," T-Roc remarked confidently.

"If you say so, but when a woman is fed up
there's no telling what she might do."

T-Roc stopped eating his food and rested
his eyes on Tracy. He was well aware that he was
playing a dangerous game, but this was the first
time somebody was calling him out on it. The very
idea of another man dicking down his wife made
T-Roc's blood boil. He was an admitted control
freak and micromanaged everything in his life
including his women. He had been married to

Chantal for so long, that he took it for granted she knew the rules and would always abide by them. His ego wouldn't allow him to believe anything differently. But now his personal assistant Tracy had him questioning himself and his marriage. It also made T-Roc wonder if his wife had finally reached her breaking point.

Chapter Six

You Already Have My Heart

"Those are some beautiful flowers," Qiana remarked when she got to work and saw the bouquet on the counter.

"Too bad they're not for me," her co-worker Margo smacked.

"I know what you mean. The hotel always has the most gorgeous arrangements."

"Those aren't hotel flowers," Margo hissed. "Those flowers are for you."

Qiana glanced over at the bouquet and then back at Margo as in disbelief. "Stop playing!"

"Trust me, I was surprised too, but I'm serious. Look at the card," Margo said, not even trying to hide how salty she was.

Qiana grabbed the card and sure enough it was addressed to her. She immediately started wondering who they could be from. "Could Robert have sent these? These look too extravagant for his taste," Qiana said talking to herself out loud.

"Who are they from?" Margo questioned being nosy, looking over Qiana's shoulder.

"No way," she mumbled covering her mouth.

"Girl, who are they from!?" Margo pressed. She was even more curious to know the identity of the sender based on Qiana's reaction.

"Genesis," Qiana finally said.

"Genesis? Who is... wait! Not that fine ass man you checked in the other day?"

"Yes! Can you believe he sent me these flowers?"

"No!" Margo shouted snatching the card out of Qiana's hand.

"What the hell are you doing?" Qiana snapped, reaching to get her card back. Margo tossed it down on the counter and walked off.

Qiana was on the verge of cursing Margo out, but stopped herself. "The audacity of that heffa," she said under her breath. It took all her restraint not to go in on Margo. But not only was she Qiana's co-worker, she was also best friends with their supervisor. Qiana desperately needed her job and wasn't about to jeopardize it because of homegirl's jealousy. Plus, Qiana was too elated about receiving the flowers from Genesis to worry about Margo's hating ass.

She stood at the front desk and debated whether she should call Genesis's room and thank him, but decided against it. The card was very generic. He simply thanked her for the nice room with the incredible view. Qiana didn't want to read more into it then end up getting her feelings hurt. So she went on about her day helping guests, but the entire time she was hoping that Genesis would show his handsome face though it never happened. For the first time, Qiana was disappointed when her shift was over. She had wanted them to request her to work later, but it didn't happen.

"Can I walk you to your car?" Qiana heard a somewhat familiar voice call out from the parking lot. She turned around to see who it was.

"Genesis!" her eyes widened and this infectious smile spread across Qiana's face.

Genesis couldn't help but to return the smile. "By the look you're giving me, I guess you're happy to see me."

"I didn't mean to make it so obvious," she said blushing.

"Don't be ashamed. I like that you're happy to see me. I'm happy to see you too. I'm assuming you're headed to your car, can I walk with you?"

"Of course... oh and thank you for the flowers. Nobody has ever given me flowers that beautiful."

"We need to change that. That should be the norm for a woman as gorgeous as you."

Qiana found herself blushing again and she was sick of it. She felt uncomfortable that a man she hardly knew was having this sort of effect on her, but she was drawn to him and refused to deny herself.

"I'm glad I ran into you before I left work. I didn't want to leave without having a chance to thank you," she said trying to regain her composure.

"Here I am. Are you headed home?" Genesis asked.

"I need to go to the grocery store first."

"Do you think you can join me for dinner before that?"

"You wanna have dinner with me?" Qiana questioned as if shocked.

"Yes, is that okay?"

"No! I mean, yes, but I don't really look that great," she said glancing down at her attire. She wasn't feeling her slacks and blouse as a first date outfit.

"I think you look perfect."

Qiana stared into Genesis's dark, deep set eyes and at that moment she realized he could tell her almost anything and she would believe it. Even if she knew it was a lie her heart would be adamant it was the truth.

"Okay, let's go have dinner."

Qiana and Genesis spent hours at a quaint Indian restaurant talking and getting to know each other. They instantly clicked as if they had been in each other's lives forever.

"I have to admit, I'm really confused."

"Confused about what?" Qiana wanted to know.

"How a woman that is beautiful and smart, with a very engaging personality isn't taken. Men in Atlanta must be slippin' because if you were in Philly or New York somebody would've put a ring on your finger a long time ago," Genesis remarked.

"Actually, I was married," she said shifting her body nervously in her chair.

"Oh really."

"Technically, I'm still married," Qiana reluctantly admitted. "But we're legally separated," she quickly added not wanting to scare off whom she was starting to think was the man of her dreams.

"I see. What man in his right mind would let you get away? If you don't mind sharing, what happened?" Genesis inquired.

Qiana let out a deep sigh. Talking about her soon to be ex-husband was probably her least favorite thing to do, but she didn't want Genesis to think she was holding anything back. She wanted to be as transparent as possible.

"Me and my husband were high school sweethearts. When we were in college I got pregnant so we decided to get married. I dropped out to be a mother and wife. In his quest to be this successful attorney his work became his mistress until he actually got him a real one. She was a paralegal at the firm he was working at."

"I'm so sorry, Qiana," Genesis said sincerely.

"The crazy part is, I heard all the horror stories of high school sweethearts getting married and it ending in divorce, but I never thought that would be me and Robert. We were best friends. My mother warned me not to drop out of college and give up my life for a man. I was so determined to prove everyone wrong that I refused to see the bullshit staring me right in the face. But when his mistress showed up at my front door saying she was pregnant with my husband's child, I couldn't deny the truth any longer. All I kept wondering was how I would tell my son and daughter that Daddy was going to give them a little brother or sister, but I wasn't the mommy."

"Damn, that's crazy. How did you tell them?" Genesis was now caught up in what sounded like a real life soap opera to him.

"His mistress ended up having a miscarriage in the beginning of her second semester. She got into a horrible car accident. She survived, but unfortunately the baby didn't."

"You sound saddened by that."

"I definitely have no love for that woman, but the baby was innocent. As a mother, I could only imagine how heartbreaking it is to lose a child. During your pregnancy you're already bonding with the child you're carrying. So yes it did sadden me, but that didn't change the state of my marriage. The damage was already done. There was no going back," Qiana made clear.

"I get it. When you find out that someone you love and thought you knew is disloyal and can't be trusted... there is no going back," Genesis stated.

"It sounds like you're speaking from experience."

"I am. I actually lost my wife. It wasn't from divorce, she was murdered."

"Ohmigoodness!" Qiana covered her mouth in dismay. "That must've been so painful."

"It was and it still is. She was pregnant with our son. But luckily, he survived. Thank God he did because I don't think I would've had the strength to live. But I didn't want my son to grow up without a mother and a father. Through him I found the will to survive. Then a woman, who started off as a business partner, became a close friend and eventually my fiancé, ended up betraying me in the worse way. I found out I was sleeping with the enemy... make that the devil."

"I thought I had it bad. You've been through hell." Qiana shook her head in disbelief.

"You don't know the half of it," Genesis scuffed, briefly reminiscing about the rollercoaster ride his life had been on. It was as if he was born into chaos and cursed to forever be in the midst of it.

"I can't even imagine. You must think my

problems are pretty boring." Qiana laughed.

"Don't make light of what you've been through. The heart is delicate and yours was broken. I do hope you'll give me a chance to mend it." Genesis reached across the table and placed his hand on top of Qiana's hand.

"I thought whatever chance I had was ruined when I confided in you about the drama in my life. Now you're asking for a chance to mend my broken heart. I must be dreaming."

"Not at all. I think we might be just what the other needs, but there's only one way to find out."

"Why me?" she questioned as if puzzled.

"Why not you?"

"I'm about to be a single mother of two. I'm in school with a part time job. With your looks alone you can have any woman you want. I'm not exactly a great catch," Qiana said sadly.

"That's where you're so wrong. Not only are you beautiful on the outside, more importantly you're beautiful on the inside. Just from talking to you, it's obvious how much you love your kids. One thing I've learned is that if a woman is good to her kids then she'll be good to me. Finally, last I checked, going to school so you can get a better job to support yourself and your kids was an admirable thing. Personally, between the two of us, I think I'm the lucky one."

Genesis smiled and completely melted Qiana's heart. She wasn't ready to admit it, but there was no need for him to try and mend her heart. Genesis already had it without even trying.

Chapter Seven

Options

"Yo, if a motherfucker call my phone one more time and hang the fuck up, I'ma change my number," Vandresse complained to Tanica as they headed home.

"Can you see the number they calling from?"

"Nope. It keep saying private. Fuck it, I ain't answering no more private calls. I usually don't, but sometime Nico be calling me from a private number and you know I ain't tryna miss his call."

"Do you think it's him calling and hanging up?" Tanica asked.

"Hell no!" Vandresse stopped in the middle of the street and turned to Tanica. "Why the fuck would he do some dumb shit like that. Plus, that nigga is way too busy to be playing them type of games. Whoever playing on my phone got too much damn time on they hand," Vandresse smacked. "Not this fuckin' shit again!" she shouted as another private call came through.

"Are you gonna answer?" Tanica wanted to know.

"That would be a negative. I ain't answering nothing private. They'll catch hint. Well damn, I didn't think it would be that fast," Vandresse commented looking down at her phone. "This has to be the same person calling back, but it's a 917 number. Hello!" Vandresse barked into the phone.

"Hoe, when I see you out in these streets I'ma fuck you up!" a female voice screamed into the phone.

Vandresse leaned back and stared at her phone like it was an unrecognizable object. "Oh, bitch you must have the wrong motherfuckin' number 'cause you can't be talkin' to me," she popped.

"I know exactly who I'm talkin' to, Vandresse!" the girl shot back. "Yo' hoish ass need to leave my man alone before I fuck you up."

"Yo' man! Who the fuck is yo' mothefuckin' man so I can whoop his ass and whoop yo' ass too!" Vandresse spit balling her fist up. She was ready to jump out her Nikes and beat a bitch down barefoot. "Hello... hello!" she kept yelling. "This trifling trick done hung up on me!" Vandresse was seething.

"Girl, what happened? Come sit down so you can calm down." Tanica walked her friend over to a bench in a nearby park. "Now tell me what happened."

"Some chick was threatening me, telling me to stay away from her man. I'm like bitch who the fuck is yo' man."

"What did she say?"

"She hung up the fuckin' phone before telling me."

"Maybe she had the wrong number, Vandresse." Tanica reasoned.

"At first I thought the same fuckin' thing until she called me by my name."

"What! She called you by your name?"

"Yes!"

"So who could it be?"

"Girl, I don't know. Courtney is my man and although Nico and I have been kicking it strong he ain't my nigga then besides him there are two other guys I've been talking to, but nothing serious. I ain't fuckin' them. They just be buying me shit in hopes they might get some pussy. Maybe one of them found my number in they man's phone and decided to act a fool. I don't fuckin' know, but that phone call got me ready to fight. I'm dressed down, my hair in a bun, I ain't wearing no makeup... this is the perfect brawl attire. A chick catch me in these streets right now, I would beat a bitch down," Vandresse scoffed, amped up.

Tanica knew Vandresse wasn't joking either. Out of the two of them, everyone always figured she was the fighter, but they had it all wrong. Visually, Vandresse had the appearance of a girl that would cry if she broke a nail. She was very polished and pretty. But Vandresse grew up around nothing but boys so she had been fighting since she was in pampers. The girl could fight like a straight up dude.

"Don't let that girl stress you out... whoever she is, she ain't worth the fight. Just let it go. Now come on," Tanica said tugging Vandresse's jacket sleeve. "Let's go home."

Vandresse frowned up her face and rolled her eyes, but after a slight protest she did get up. "You right. I got better things to think about. Like gettin' off this bench 'cause Courtney is picking me up at seven. I need to get home and get dressed. So fuck that bitch." Vandresse playfully twisted her neck and laughed before Tanica joined in. The two best friends smiled at each other, cuffed their arms together, and walked off.

"You been missing a lot lately," was the first thing

Courtney said when Vandresse got in the car.

"No 'damn baby, you look good tonight in them jeans' or 'my weave is tight, my lip gloss is poppin'. None of that just some, 'you been missing lately'," Vandresse hissed putting her seatbelt on.

"That ain't the point. I shouldn't have to chase my girl down especially since everything you got on I probably paid for," Courtney barked gunning it down the street.

"So where we eating tonight, 'cause I'm starving," Vandresse said choosing to ignore Courtney's slick mouth. Originally she had planned on grilling him about the phone call she got earlier, but with his foul mood she decided now wasn't the time.

"We have to wait on the food. There's another spot I need to hit first."

"What spot is that 'cause I'm starving."

"I told you I got this artist I'm tryna break into the music business. He's meeting me over at the studio right now for a potential major break. So just sit back," Courtney said sounding annoyed.

Vandresse glanced over at Courtney. She wanted to dig her nails into his buttery deep reddish brown skin and draw blood. She was growing tired of his funky attitude. It was as if what Vandresse wanted or thought didn't matter because Courtney had everything and she relied on him. She was becoming frustrated with the dynamics of their relationship, but Vandresse wasn't ready to call it quits just yet. Despite the fact she knew he was seeing mad other chicks, but yet wanted to regulate her like his paid for property, she felt at the moment he was her best option. So for now, Vandresse would remain quiet and play her role until a better option presented itself.

"Come on," Courtney said when he pulled up in front of the studio on West 49th street. During the ride up the elevator, all Vandresse kept thinking was how she hoped this would be a quick session and they would be right back out the door. That was until they entered the studio and to her surprise, the hottest new rapper on the scene was behind the mic.

"That's Supreme! How do you know him?" Vandresse questioned not even caring she sounded like a bonafide fan in front of her man.

"I don't. I'm mad cool wit' his manager. We

go way back and he's doing me a huge favor."

"Wait, he's gonna let that artist you were talking about be on a record with Supreme?" Vandresse couldn't contain her excitement at the possibility of being right.

"Exactly! I told you this was a major break. So go have a seat while I go do a little politicking." Courtney headed inside the booth while Vandresse sat down and observed.

She fidgeted with her phone about sending Tanica a text. *Nah, don't do it, Vandresse. Just chill. But damn, I can't wait to tell her I'm in the studio with none other than Supreme. This nigga even finer in person*, she thought shaking her head.

Vandresse then pulled out her makeup compact and tried to check her makeup discreetly not wanting to be noticed, at least not yet. The moment she walked in the studio and laid eyes on Supreme, Vandresse had begun plotting on a takeover. She wanted him and it was as simple as that. In her mind, the fact they were in such close proximity meant she was being giving a rare opportunity and needed to seize it.

How the fuck am I gonna get this dude's attention without coming across as a desperate groupie? Hmmm, I have to figure that out before making my move. Supreme ain't some hood rich nigga that would simply be impressed with a pretty face and phat ass. That's probably being thrown his way on a regular basis. I have to be slick with it, Vandresse reasoned, continuing to plot as she sat on the couch in the sitting area of the studio.

"Come on, let's go," Courtney said disrupting Vandresse's thoughts as he came out the studio.

"We're leaving so soon?" Vandresse asked doing her best not to sound as devastated as she was feeling at the moment.

"I thought you'd be happy given how hungry you said you were," Courtney sniped.

"I am happy, just surprised. I figured I would have to wait awhile since you said you were politicking and all," Vandresse smirked.

"It's all good. Before I got here Supreme listened to my artist and he gave it the green light to have him sing the hook on the track. He's gonna lay down the vocals next week so my job here is done," Courtney explained.

"Cool. Then let's go because a bitch is starving," Vandresse said giggling. She waited until they were almost to the car when she said,

"Oh my fuckin' goodness!" she yelled digging through her purse.

"What's wrong?" Courtney asked unlocking the car door.

"I must've left my phone in the women's bathroom. I used it while I was waiting for you," she lied. "Fuck!"

"Well, you better go get it," Courtney huffed. "You always forgettin' some shit," he mumbled.

"I'll be right back." When Vandresse turned around and headed back inside with a wide grin on her face. "First part down, next step to go."

As Vandresse rode up in the elevator she dabbed on some more lip gloss, fluffed out her weave, tightened up her bra to make sure the girls were sitting perky and pretty and made sure her jeans were accentuating the gap between her thighs. By the time the elevator stopped she believed everything was in check. She headed straight to the studio on a mission.

Gosh, luck sure is on my side. Vandresse smiled to herself when she entered the studio and Supreme was coming out. Instead of Vandresse making eye contact with the rapper she went over to the couch she was sitting on and pretended to be looking frantically for her phone. Pretending because she knew exactly where it was: behind the middle throw pillow. When Courtney had said it was time for them to go, she had quickly come up with a remedy for an excuse to come back to the studio.

"Can I help you with something?" Supreme asked to Vandresse's relief. It was mandatory that he speak to her first or her plan would be a bust.

"Do you work here... did anyone turn in a cell phone? Because I was just in here less than ten minutes ago and I can't find it," Vandresse said sounding exasperated.

"Nah, I don't work here," Supreme said chuckling as if amused that the young lady thought he worked for the studio instead of being there to record his upcoming album.

"Oh, okay then, excuse me because I need to get back to looking for my phone," she said being super dismissive.

Supreme was about to walk out, but a combination of his ego being slightly hurt because the woman was paying him no mind and the fact she was a gorgeous woman had Supreme feeling some type of way. "I can help you... look for your phone that is," Supreme offered.

"You don't have to do that," Vandresse countered, still not giving Supreme any attention, which was working in her favor, just as she hoped. All while pushing her phone even further down behind the pillow.

"I really don't mind." Supreme walked over to Vandresse and she could smell his cologne.

Damn, I love a nigga that smell good, she closed her eyes thinking to herself.

"Maybe it fell on the floor." Vandresse sighed out loud, bending over as if looking under the couch. Only a blind man wouldn't notice how she had curves in all the right places. Supreme did his best not to look, but there was no denying her sex appeal.

"Are you sure you left it in here?" he questioned.

"Definitely! This is the last place I had it." Vandresse glanced up and locked eyes with Supreme for the first time. She gave him this deer caught in the headlight stare. With those glossy lips poppin' he ate it up.

"Since I'm helping you find your phone you

can at least tell me your name," Supreme said.

"Vandresse and yours?"

"Supreme."

"I appreciate you helping me, but I understand if you have better things to do."

"No, I'm good. But I know a way you can make it worth my time."

"How's that?" She gave Supreme a flirtatious smile.

"If I find your phone you'll give me your number."

"First, let's find my phone and then I'll think about it," she smirked. "Wait! Do you hear that?"

"No, I don't hear anything." Supreme shook his head.

"Listen carefully, my phone is vibrating."

Supreme leaned closer in Vandresse's direction. "Yeah, I do hear it," he said nodding. "I think it's coming from over here." Supreme was right in the vicinity. Instead of joining in the search, Vandresse remained on bended knee wanting Supreme to be the phone hero.

"Found it!" Supreme grinned. "You know what that means."

"Yeah, it means you found my phone. Now

give it here!" Vandresse grabbed for it, but Supreme lifted his arm up high so she couldn't reach it. "Give me my phone!" she said giggling.

"Not until you give me those digits," Supreme replied, playfully swinging his arm in the air. "Give me your number or no phone. It's up to you."

Vandresse continued to play his little game for a couple more minutes until she acted as if Supreme had wore her down and she finally relented. "Fine! You can have my number now give me my damn phone!" she snapped. Vandresse couldn't help but think all this scheming was even more fun than she thought it would be.

"Now was that so bad?" Supreme questioned after putting Vandresse's number in his phone.

"I won't know the answer to that until after you call," she said winking. "But I gotta go. My ride is waiting on me." Vandresse winked again and then headed out.

I did it! I did it! Vandresse was screaming to herself as she walked away from Supreme. She then looked down at her phone to see the missed call assuming it was Courtney that had called her, wondering what was taking so long, but it was Nico. A wide smile crept across her face and she was tempted to call him back, but didn't want to press her luck when it came to keeping Courtney waiting. She was ready to dump him, but until she could lock down Nico or even better Supreme, Vandresse decided to deal.

Chapter Eight

Time To Move On

"You were amazing," Lorenzo said sprinkling kisses down the spine of Chantal's back.

"Not as amazing as you. You have this way of fucking my mind and body before you even enter inside of me," Chantal purred as her naked body slithered on the silk sheets while turning to face Lorenzo.

"Just like that you got me hard again. I bet you still wet." Lorenzo gently spread Chantal's legs, ready to slide right back inside.

"Baby, I wish I could do it again," she said pressing her lips against his. "But I have to go. I'm already late."

"Late for what?"

"Today is my wedding anniversary and my husband made dinner plans for us. I should've been home getting ready, but instead I've been locked up in this hotel room with you all day."

Lorenzo rolled off Chantal and looked up at the chandelier fixture in his hotel suite. He had conveniently made himself forget Chantal was married for the last few months they had been seeing each other, but when your lover is naked in bed with you and says she has to go home to her husband, you can't lie to yourself even if you want to.

"I'll be back tomorrow," Chantal said leaning over to kiss him before getting out of bed.

"I have something to do." Lorenzo turned his head so she couldn't kiss him.

Chantal stepped out of the bed and began gathering her clothes. "It's not like you didn't know I was married," she stated slipping on her violet lace bra and panties.

You can't dispute facts and Lorenzo couldn't deny that what Chantal said was the truth. He had willingly embarked in a sexual relationship with a married woman. He initially believed they would have a very brief affair and after a few times of great sex his infatuation would subside then move on. But that didn't happen. After all this time Lorenzo was still infatuated with Chantal. She had this fire about her as if she was slightly dangerous, crazy, or maybe both. Whatever it was, it turned Lorenzo on and made the sex incredible. The fact that she was married which made her unattainable also played into Lorenzo's attraction to Chantal. He didn't like feeling this way.

"I don't think we need to see each other anymore," Lorenzo stated coldly.

Chantal stopped buttoning up her blouse and turned to face Lorenzo. "You don't mean that."

"Yes, I do. It was fun while it lasted, but it's time we both moved on."

"Fun while it lasted... and to think I thought we shared something special. I guess the joke is on me," Chantal scoffed, quickly putting on the rest of her clothes and grabbing her purse to leave.

"Chantal, wait!" Lorenzo called out, regretting what he told her.

"Don't bother. You've said enough." Chantal slammed the door and left.

Chantal sat playing with her food replaying the words that were exchanged between her and Lorenzo earlier. He had been the only bright spot in her troubled life and she had no idea what to do now that he was out of it.

"This is your favorite restaurant and you've barely touched your food. What's going on with you tonight? We're supposed to be celebrating our anniversary not acting like we just left a funeral," T-Roc observed.

"I have a lot on my mind that's all," Chantal said putting down her fork and taking another sip of her champagne.

"All you do is dress and rest. What the fuck could you have on your mind? Wait... dress, rest, and go to the gym," he added sarcastically.

Chantal rolled her eyes and continued sipping her champagne before picking her fork back up. With a subtle gesture she then began stabbing the beef tataki imagining it was her husband's throat.

"No slick comeback?" T-Roc questioned glancing over at this wife who was keeping her cool.

"Why bother... I need a manicure," Chantal commented offhandedly while she studied her nails.

T-Roc gave his wife a quizzical look. "Here, I got you something. Happy Anniversary." He put a Harry Winston jewelry box on the table.

Chantal took her time opening the blue burl wood collectors watch box in blue lacquered finish. "This is pretty," she remarked, closing the box.

"That's all you got is, this is pretty. What the fuck is wrong wit' you!" he barked.

"What the fuck is wrong with you!" Chantal snapped back even louder causing people in the restaurant to stare. "You think you can buy me another piece of jewelry? Am I supposed to be what... grateful? Get the fuck outta here! Why don't you recycle this bullshit gift and give it to one of your mistresses. I'm sure they would be suuuuper pleased," she hissed.

"Keep your voice down," T-Roc demanded.

"Why? I'm sure at least half the women in here are dealing with the same BS so I'm in good company," she sneered.

"You're drunk. We need to go home," T-Roc stated before calling for the waiter to immediately bring the check.

"What's the rush... am I embarrassing you," Chantal mocked. "I guess it must be so disappointing having me as a wife instead of that prude Tyler Blake you chased after like a lovesick puppy. But she didn't want you!" Chantal laughed loudly now drinking the champagne straight from the bottle.

"Give me that!" T-Roc reached out trying to yank the bottle out of Chantal's hand, but he wasn't fast enough. She had scooted her body over and continued laughing hysterically, loving that she was getting under her husband's skin.

"Poor tink tink. I know you wanna slap the shit outta me so bad, but you know these uppity folks ain't gonna allow you to fuck up they establishment," Chantal said giggling. "If they even think you might lay a hand on me, they'll have the police come put them handcuffs on you before you can even get your lawyer on the phone."

"If you don't shut up and walk out this restaurant with me right now, it's gonna take more than New York's finest to save you," T-Roc warned.

Chantal was drunk and high from snorting a line of coke when she went to the ladies room earlier, but she was lucid enough to recognize that look on T-Roc's face and the tone of his voice. She didn't need to push him any further.

"I see it's becoming harder for you to take a joke. I guess with age you're starting to lose your sense of humor." Chantal took the last sip of her drink, grabbed her purse and stood up. With swiftness T-Roc leaped over to her side and took Chantal's hand. He was pissed with his wife, but he also didn't want her to fall on her ass in the middle of the ultra exclusive restaurant. T-Roc held onto Chantal tightly as they made their way to the awaiting car.

Chantal woke up the next day with a throbbing headache. At first she couldn't even remember what happened the night before that was causing her head to feel like it was about to explode. She reached over and opened the drawer on the nightstand to get some aspirin. Chantal swallowed them with no water and was about to lay her head back down when she heard her phone ringing. Her eyes lit up when she saw it was Lorenzo. Before answering she got up and looked around to make sure T-Roc wasn't in the bedroom.

"Hello."

"I didn't think you were gonna answer," Lorenzo said.

"I didn't think you were gonna call."

"How was dinner last night?"

"Based on how my head felt when I woke up, I would say horrible."

"I can't say that I'm disappointed to hear that."

"I should've never mentioned my anniversary," Chantal said. "It was insensitive."

"Why don't you make it up to me."

"How can I do that?"

"Come see me."

"I thought you said you never wanted to see me again," Chantal said.

"I lied. So are you coming?" Lorenzo asked.

"I'm on the way." Chantal couldn't hang the phone up fast enough and get in the shower. Being with Lorenzo was all her body yearned for.

"Mom, you're up!" Justina beamed when Chantal came into the kitchen.

"Yes, why do you sound so surprised?" Chantal questioned while getting one of her organic green juices out of the refrigerator.

"Dad told me not to disturb you. He said you had a little bit too much to drink last night and would probably be asleep for most of the day."

"Oh, how considerate of your father, but as you can see I'm fine."

"Where are you going?"

"Yeah, where are you going?" T-Roc walked into the kitchen and asked as if he was about to interrogate his wife.

"To a yoga class... duh. Can't you all tell by the leggings and tank top I have on," Chantal said shrugging. During her shower, Chantal had already come up with her cover story in case she was questioned and dressed for it too.

"I should've known. You don't have that ridiculous bod for nothing," Justina said winking.

"Justina, why don't you join your mother for her yoga class? I'm sure she would enjoy your company. Wouldn't you, Chantal?"

"Of course I would!" Chantal lied, taking a large gulp of her juice.

"I would love to, but I'm about to meet Aaliyah and Amir for lunch. Maybe next time." Justina smiled kissing her mom and dad goodbye then heading out.

"I guess I should be going too," Chantal said anxious to get to Lorenzo.

"Before you go, Chantal, I wanna discuss what happened last night." T-Roc stepped in Chantal's way blocking her path.

"I had too much to drink and got a little carried away."

"It was more than that. I want to know what's going on with you and I want to know now," T-Roc demanded.

"Can we do this later. I have a lot of stress I need to burn off and this class is the only thing that will relieve it," Chantal said sweetly.

"You go 'head to your class, but this conversation isn't over. We'll finish discussing it when I get back home tonight."

"Whatever you say, baby." Chantal smiled in that same sugary sweet voice. T-Roc watched with suspicion as his wife happily skipped out the door. He couldn't figure out what was going on with her. He wondered if she was popping some new pills that put her in an upbeat mood and then the idea of her having an affair crossed his mind. But as fast as it came it went. T-Roc wouldn't even allow himself to give that notion more then a second of his time. In his mind, Chantal wouldn't even have the audacity to cheat on him. I mean who could be a better catch than T-Roc or so he believed.

Chapter Nine

Can't Let You Go

"What you over there daydreaming about... I should say who!" Margo smacked. "That nigga got you so open, you can't even concentrate at work."

"I'm not neglecting my job. Look around, there's nobody here," Qiana smacked back wishing she was using her hand on Margo instead of her mouth.

"Well, you still seem out of it and that isn't very professional when you're working the front desk."

"Oh and it's professional of you to inquire about my personal life by saying a nigga got me open? Hmmm!"

"Don't get mad at me because you not doing your job because you too focused on some dude."

"What is your problem with me, Margo? You always have something smart to say, especially when it comes to Genesis."

"Because ever since you started dating him you act like you too good for this job. I've seen the new clothes, jewelry, and I heard about the fancy restaurants he's been taking you to. If you think you're such hot shit, why don't you just quit," Margo popped, pointing her finger in Qiana's direction.

"You so pressed about my relationship. It must suck being so damn jealous!"

"Jealous of what? You've only been dating him for the last few months and he always in and out of town. He don't even live here," Margo said twisting her thick neck. "He probably got a wife and kids back in New York. All while you sitting here at work waiting for your so-called man to come back to see you. So again I ask, jealous of what?"

Before Qiana could respond she noticed a hotel guest approaching the desk so both women put on fake smiles to hide their disdain for each other. Qiana watched as Margo helped the guest and she couldn't help but think about what her co-worker had just said. She would never admit it to Margo, but she had fallen hard for Genesis and him living out of town made her somewhat insecure. Although he did his best to make Qiana feel special, she did wonder what he was doing and who he was seeing when he went back home. As her mind began drifting off again she finally got the call she had been waiting for.

"Hey, handsome."

Genesis could hear Qiana smiling through the phone.

"Hello, my beautiful. What are you doing?"

"At work thinking about how much I miss you."

"I miss you, too. I'll be able to show you just

how much in about three hours."

"Omigosh! You're here?" Qiana couldn't contain her excitement. She lowered her voice when she caught Margo glancing in her direction. "Are you?" she asked again wanting to make sure before getting too happy.

"Yep. I'm just leaving my hotel room. I have to go meet with a business associate and then I was coming to pick you up. Will you be off of work by then?" Genesis wanted to know.

"Yes, I will and it can't happen soon enough. I hate that you don't stay at this hotel anymore. Then I wouldn't have to wait to see you."

"I know, but we both agreed it was better for me to start staying somewhere else when we started getting serious," Genesis reminded her.

"I know, especially with how nosey my co-workers are, but I still hate it. I miss sneaking up in your hotel room during my break for a quickie. But the quickie always turned into so much more." Qiana giggled remembering how perfect Genesis always felt inside of her.

"Don't worry, after dinner you'll be coming back to the room with me."

"Why don't we skip going out and just do

room service. You have everything I need."

"Say no more. I'll see you in a few hours."

"Great! But pick me up from home instead of work. I wanna change into something nice for you."

"Will do, baby," Genesis said before hanging up.

On his drive over to see Mateo, Genesis cracked a smile knowing Qiana would be sharing his bed tonight. They had grown close over the past few months and it felt good to have a woman back in his life on a romantic level. After Chanel's betrayal, Genesis began to think he would never be able to open his heart to another woman again. Then Qiana came into his life and he was starting to believe he had a chance at love again.

Imagining a future with Qiana had Genesis in an upbeat mood. So much so, his natural paranoid persona had taken a back seat. So when he thought he saw a car following him to Mateo's house, he brushed it off and continued on his way.

"I wasn't expecting you to return so soon," Mateo said, greeting Genesis at the door. "I'm very impressed."

"My customers are very impressed with your product. You said it was the best so I shouldn't be surprised."

"I stand by my products. All my drugs are one hundred percent pure. Only the best indeed," Mateo boasted. "Please have a seat. Can I get you anything?"

"No, I'm good but thanks," Genesis said nodding.

"Listen, this is your sixth time coming back in a very short period of time. You are making me a lot of money." Mateo clapped his hands together in enthusiasm. "You have far exceeded my expectations, Genesis, and I would like to show you my gratitude."

"Mateo, I wanted this business arrangement to be a positive experience for both of us."

"Me, too. Especially given the duplicity I received from my last buyer. But you have proven to be a man of your word and for that you will be rewarded. I will be implementing an additional twenty percent price reduction on all your future orders including the one today."

"Are you serious?!" Genesis's mouth dropped as he began calculating the enormous profit he would be making.

"I never joke about my money or my drugs. You have become a great asset and I want us to have a long and profitable relationship. I hope this gesture proves that," Mateo said winking.

"It does and greatly appreciated. I won't let you down," Genesis said, standing up to shake Mateo's hand.

"Damn, how are we supposed to go out to dinner when I'll be spending the entire time imagining taking that dress off of you." Genesis pulled Qiana into his arms, as they stood in the middle of her living room.

"I'm glad you like it since you picked it out," Qiana said giggling.

"I picked that out?" Genesis slowly twirled Qiana around. "I have good taste." He chuckled, admiring the dreamy emerald-colored wrap dress that featured a thigh high split, twist over front, and lightweight satin fabric.

"Yes, you do," she said tilting her head to kiss him. "But you'll have to wait to take this dress off of me because I'm starving."

"That makes two of us. Let's get outta here," Genesis said opening the front door for Qiana.

"So how did your business meeting go today?" Qiana inquired once they had settled in the car and headed to the restaurant.

"Even better than I expected. So good that I wanted to run something past you."

"What is it?" Qiana turned to Genesis curious to hear what he had to say.

"You mentioned a few weeks ago that since your divorce is final, you and the kids had to move out the house."

"Without Robert living there, I can't afford the house and even if I could I need a fresh start. I've been looking at some really cute apartments that I think will be perfect for me and the kids."

"I'll be coming to Atlanta a lot more for business and I thought maybe it was time I got a house here."

"Really! That would be fantastic. I'd love to see you more. I always miss you when you're gone."

"I always miss you too," Genesis admitted. "I wouldn't be here a lot so the house would be more for you and the kids."

"Excuse me?" Qiana had a puzzled look on her face.

"Instead of you moving into an apartment, I wanna buy a house for you and your kids and when I come to town, maybe you wouldn't mind if I stay sometimes," Genesis joked.

"I would want you to stay all the time, but don't play with me like this, Genesis," Qiana said becoming stern.

"I'm not playing. Things are going really good between us and so is my business. My woman should benefit from that. I want you to have a nice home and you deserve it."

"I don't know what to say. You've already been so good to me. I've never had a man treat me as kind as you have. Now a house." Qiana exhaled and looked up as if her life couldn't get any more perfect.

"This is only the beginning." Genesis stopped in front of the restaurant and leaned over placing his lips softly on hers before giving his keys to the valet.

Qiana held onto Genesis not wanting to let him go. They walked hand in hand towards the entrance and she felt like she was living a dream that quickly turned into a nightmare.

Pop... pop... pop!!!!

Initially the sound was similar to the sharp crack produced by a bullwhip so Qiana was startled, but had no clue the severity of the situation. On the other hand, Genesis was no stranger to dodging bullets so he immediately went into protective mode. He flung his body over Qiana, lunging their bodies behind a nearby car.

Right before Genesis used his body to shield Qiana, she caught a glimpse of the valet being riddled with bullets. She screamed out in horror as the blood appeared to explode from every inch of his body.

"Stay down," Genesis stated to Qiana calmly. He could feel her shaking underneath him. A few moments later the barrage of bullets ceased just as quickly as they had began. "Are you okay?" Genesis questioned lifting Qiana's face.

"No, I'm not," she said as her bottom lip trembled. "What just happened? Was someone trying to kill the valet guy?" Qiana asked, trying to wrap her mind around how they had gotten caught in the middle of a drive-by shooting.

"I doubt it. Those bullets were meant for me and the valet was in the wrong place at the wrong time," Genesis admitted without hesitation.

When Genesis made that affirmation, Qiana knew that was a clear sign she needed to bolt. No man was worth risking her life over; at least that's what her mind told her, but she was listening to her heart. Qiana was in too deep and she refused to let Genesis go.

Chapter Ten

Be Your Girl

"I'm sorry I've been MIA. I've been in and out of town a lot lately."

"I understand you making moves out here in these streets." Vandresse smiled at Nico.

"I am, but I still wanna make it up to you."

"You already have," Vandresse said stretching her arms. "That was the best sex we've ever had."

She giggled turning over and straddling her body on top of Nico. "I can tell you missed me and so did he," she teased as she positioned herself to slide Nico's hardened dick back inside of her.

"I can't get enough of you," Nico moaned as Vandresse rode his dick like she was in a race to win the top prize. His fingertips caressed the nipples of her firm breasts as Vandresse arched her back relishing in the pleasure Nico was bringing her. The sex continued to intensify until they both reached their climax and Vandresse's body collapsed on top of Nico.

"That was incredible," she gushed kissing Nico's neck.

"You get all the credit on that," Nico said pressing his hands deeply into Vandresse's soft yet tight ass. "I think it might be time for you to leave that other nigga alone."

Vandresse gave Nico a mischievous grin before lying down beside him. "Does that mean you'll leave all those other chicks alone and make me your only girl?"

"What other chicks?" He shrugged coolly.

"Whatever, nigga." Vandresse playfully hit Nico on the chest. "I heard about you and your player ways, but I have a man so I can't really say shit. But I ain't gonna lie, I've caught real feelings for you."

"It wasn't the plan, but I have feelings for you too. That's why I'm tryna lock you down."

"I would definitely cut Courtney loose if I thought there was a chance we could be in an exclusive relationship. But Nico Carter, you ain't gon' have me in these streets lookin' crazy. I have a reputation to keep intact," Vandresse smirked.

"I feel you, Ma. I ain't exactly the exclusive type, but I will make you my number one. You think you have a reputation now, you become my girl and I'll have every borough in New York bowing down to you," Nico said with confidence.

"That's why I love you, 'cause you always know exactly what to say to keep my pussy wet," Vandresse purred, ready for round three.

Courtney was lying in the bed knocked out

when his baby mama, LaQuisha decided to take advantage of the slumber he was in. She had been paying close attention when he would unlock his phone and was able to figure out his code. She had been patiently waiting for the perfect opportunity to put it to use and it had finally presented itself. When LaQuisha came across Vandresse's contact information she knew she had hit pay dirt. She read through all the text exchanges including the one where Vandresse was demanding a nice chunk of change from Courtney to get some new furniture for her apartment. That shit made LaQuisha's blood boil especially since getting funds from her baby daddy was like pulling teeth. Courtney had no problem buying shit for the baby, but when it came to LaQuisha, he was unwilling to give her a dime.

So this who you giving your coins to, LaQuisha thought to herself as she glared at a sleeping Courtney. *You laying up in here with me in my old ass bed, but you giving this hoe money to furnish her damn apartment. Hell no! That bitch gotta go*!

The more LaQuisha read through the text messages, the angrier she became. She then peeped photos of Vandresse posing with

Courtney and solo like she thought she was cute. The more angry LaQuisha got, the more she was tempted to wake Courtney up and cuss his ass out, but decided not to bite the hand that fed her, even though she was nibbling on crumbs. But as far as LaQuisha was concerned something was better than nothing especially since Courtney wasn't even her man. But if things went the way LaQuisha planned, she would get rid of all of Courtney's other chicks and be the last bitch standing.

"Girl, you gon' get enough of juggling all these men," Tanica said shaking her head as she sat down on the sofa. "You were with Courtney a few days ago, then Nico, now you about to go hang out with Supreme. I don't know whether to be jealous or worried about yo' safety," Tanica continued as she turned the channels on the television.

"Listen, I got this," Vandresse said as she

put the finishing touches on a lace front wig she was making. "Plus, I should be able to get rid of Courtney pretty soon."

"But Courtney is the one that's paying the bills and got us all this new furniture for the crib. You can't get rid of him!"

"Yes, I can if I can get a better replacement."

"I hope you don't think you about to lock Supreme down?!" Tanica scoffed. "I mean, no doubt you bad and mad niggas be checking for you, but Supreme ain't the average dude. He like the hottest new rapper out. He got access to way too much pussy to settle down wit' you. You my girl, but I'm just tryna keep it real."

Vandresse stopped sewing the last track on the wig cap and glanced up at Tanica. "Didn't nobody say I was gonna lock down Supreme!" she snapped. Pissed that her best friend doubted her power of persuasion over a man, even if that man just happened to be fine, rich, and famous.

"You just said that you was about to get rid of Courtney. I assumed you was tryna make Supreme his replacement."

"You assumed wrong," Vandresse said rolling her eyes. "I ain't gon' front and act like that wouldn't be the ideal come up, but I'm not stupid. I know I would have to put in a lot of time and work to lock a nigga like Supreme down, but don't question my skills because the shit can be done."

"Why don't you do it then?" Tanica shot back, liking the fact that for the first time Vandresse was feeling a little insecure when it came to a man.

"Truth be told, I ain't in the position for all that."

"What the hell does that mean?" Tanica frowned.

Vandresse let out a long sigh as if she wasn't in the mood to explain this shit to Tanica, but did so anyway. "You can't come at a dude like Supreme asking him to buy you expensive shit, pay your bills, and ice you out. You have to be able to maintain and look the part of a bad bitch to get his attention, but you also have to be able to finance that shit too. I can't afford that. That's why I need a man to finance my situation until I can get Supreme to fall for me."

"You might as well stay with Courtney while you tryna work your magic on Supreme and stop wasting your time with Nico," Tanica suggested.

"The thing is, I really like Nico and he is so fuckin' good in bed," Vandresse said smiling, thinking about their last sex session.

"But you already in wit' Courtney and he ain't got no problem spending that dough on you."

"True, but I think Nico make more paper than Courtney. I just haven't asked him to trick on me because like I said, I'm really digging dude. Plus, I'm sick of Courtney's whorish ass."

"Oh, like Nico ain't a whore too," Tanica said shrugging. "Girl, you about to jump from bad to worse. You need to—"

"Shut up for a minute and let me answer this call," Vandresse snapped, tired of hearing Tanica's voice. "Hello!"

"Bitch, I told you to leave my man alone. This my last time warning you!" the girl barked.

"Who the fuck is this? You doing a lot of yappin', but ain't droppin' no names. Who the fuck is yo' man?'

"Yo' hoe ass must be fuckin' a lot of niggas if you don't know who my man is."

"Girl, bye! I don't have time for this dumb shit. Either speak up or shut the fuck up!"

"Stop acting like you don't know Courtney is my man."

"Oh, really! So how long you been wit' Courtney?"

"Long enough to know he sick of yo' ass and his silly baby mama."

"Excuse me, did you say baby mama? Now I know you playin' on my phone 'cause Courtney ain't got no baby."

"Oh, you don't know about Kiana, his three month old daughter? Like I said, leave my man alone. He don't want you!"

"If he don't want me then why are you calling my phone?"

"Because I'm pregnant that's why!"

"So Courtney already has a baby and now he has another one on the way. That's what you telling me?"

"Yes!" the girl said proudly.

"You still ain't told me your name," Vandresse stated.

"Brie," she smacked.

"I'll tell you what, Brie. I'ma give you what you want. I'm done wit' Courtney. He is all yours so don't call my phone no more." Vandresse slammed down her phone pissed. "I told you that nigga was whorish."

"Hold up, Courtney got a baby and a girlfriend?" Tanica had been all up in Vandresse's conversation, but wanted confirmation.

"Yes! I knew he was cheating, but this..." Vandresse couldn't even finish her thought she was so upset.

"Maybe the girl is lying. You need to call Courtney and ask him," Tanica advised.

"I ain't asking him shit. That girl wasn't lying. Let's say she ain't pregnant, why would she lie about him having a baby with some other chick?"

"So you just gonna let it go and not say nothing?"

"Hanging out with Supreme at the studio is my priority right now, so I need to get dressed." Vandresse stood up grabbing her wig. "I'll figure out how to handle Courtney's trifling ass later," she promised before storming off.

Chapter Eleven

Love Is My New Drug

Tracy was finishing up a lunch meeting at the Mandarin Oriental Hotel when she noticed Chantal walking through the lobby. At first she figured her boss's wife was there to get pampered at the spa, but when she walked past that entrance and instead headed to the elevators, Tracy started thinking something else.

She hurried through the lobby trying to catch up with Chantal, but by the time she reached the elevator she was already gone.

Hmmm, who is Chantal visiting at a hotel in the middle of the afternoon.... could Chantal be here seeing another man, Tracy pondered while walking out. Seeing Chantal had sparked her interest and she wondered if her boss had any idea that his wife was here. If he didn't, Tracy was about to make it her business to let him know.

"Baby, do I have to go so soon," Angela said still kissing on T-Roc.

"Yeah, I have a lot of work to do. I'ma call you later on," he said stroking her hair as he rushed her out the door.

"You promise?" Angela was now licking on T-Roc's ear as he was opening the door, in an attempt to arouse him so they could go back upstairs and have sex again. When Angela felt

T-Roc's hardened dick to her delight she knew it was working. "Close the door and let's go back to bed," she whispered seductively.

Without warning, the door flew open startling both Angela and T-Roc. "Who the fuck is she!" Harper yelled, shoving Angela away from T-Roc, which caused her to trip and fall down on the marble floor. Before Angela even had a chance to regain her composure, Harper grabbed her hair and started to drag her near the wood-burning fireplace.

"Harper, that's enough!" T-Roc barked trying to contain his out of control lover. He was stunned that such a slim woman had so much strength, but Harper's jealous rage gave her the power of a madman.

Angela was doing her best to fight off the crazy woman, but once Harper got a hold of her neck, she was gripping it like a pitbull.

"What the hell is going on in here?!" Tracy yelled out when she entered T-Roc's crib. It was complete mayhem.

"Tracy, come help me get Harper off Angela," T-Roc ordered. At this point Harper was so zoned out he would have to physically assault her to break the fight up and T-Roc wasn't willing to do that.

"I am not getting in the middle of that dumb shit." Tracy stood firm with her arms folded.

"Tracy, please! I can't put my hands on this woman. I might fuck around and accidentally hurt her."

"Nope! Them yo' hoes, you fix it!" Tracy popped back not budging.

"I'll double your paycheck this month."

"Triple it and we have a deal."

"Fine! Now can you get over here!"

Tracy kicked off her stilettos and ran up on Harper who was damn near about to strangle Angela to death. Tracy decided her best option was to put Harper in a headlock since she was already down on the floor. After a few seconds of cutting off her air supply, Harper let go of her grip on Angela and seemed to slip back into reality.

"I'm calling the police! I'm having you arrested for attempted murder!" Angela screamed out when she was finally able to stand up. She ran to get her cell phone from her purse.

"I can't let you do that." T-Roc grabbed Angela's purse with the swiftness.

"Give me my purse! That woman's crazy... she belongs in jail!" Angela was furious and T-Roc couldn't blame her, but there was no way he was letting her call the police. If the press got a hold of this story he would never hear the end of it. T-Roc would be on the front page of the *New York Post* and *Daily News* every day until they dissected his entire personal life.

"Tracy, watch Harper while I talk to Angela privately." T-Roc took her by the hand while she continued to scream and curse in her Spanish language, which he noticed she did whenever she got upset.

"I got this!" Tracy yelled out keeping both eyes on Harper.

"Angela, baby, I need you to relax. It's hard for me to talk to you when you're upset like this."

"That woman needs to be in jail. Do you see what she did... she tried to kill me."

"Harper was completely out of line and she will be dealt with. But I can't let you call the police. You know that I'm married. I can't let what happened here get out."

"What about me, T-Roc? What about what I've been through."

"You're right," T-Roc said walking over to his desk to retrieve his checkbook. "I think this should be more than enough to cover any inconvenience you endured today."

When T-Roc handed the check over to Angela, her eyes lit up as if saying that dragging she endured was well worth it for all these zeros. "Thank you, baby," she said giving him a kiss. "You know this doesn't change anything between us. I still want to keep seeing you," she said smiling.

"I know. I'll call you. Let me walk you out." T-Roc led Angela out, holding her hand and knowing this was the last time he would be seeing her. He kissed her sweetly on the lips before she walked out the door. T-Roc was so smooth with it, Angela had no clue that he was kissing her goodbye for good. When T-Roc came back into the living room, Harper was siting in a corner wiping away tears as if she was the victim.

"I don't know where you be getting these bat shit crazy women from, but you need to get your shit together before things turn deadly," Tracy warned.

"I apologize for getting you caught up in the middle of this. But I am glad you showed up when you did. Why did you come over?" T-Roc questioned.

Tracy hesitated for a moment. The real reason she showed up was to tell her boss that she suspected his wife was seeing another man. But after what she walked in on, Tracy changed her mind. T-Roc was being reckless with his love life and she didn't want to add to the madness by revealing that more than likely, Chantal was having an affair of her own. Tracy decided for the time being she would keep her mouth shut.

"I just wanted to talk to you about the meeting I had earlier today. No big deal, we can discuss it later. You need to go deal with Harper."

"Yeah, you're right."

"Do you need me to stay?"

"No, I think I can handle things from here. Thanks again, Tracy. I owe you."

"You always do. I know we joke a lot, but I'm serious. You really need to reevaluate your personal life. Juggling all these women, especially when you have a wife at home, is a recipe for disaster. Don't say I didn't warn you," were Tracy's departing words.

"I think I'm falling in love with you," Chantal looked over at Lorenzo and said as they lay in bed together, eating strawberries and drinking champagne.

"Do you mean that or are you only saying it because when I'm inside of you we create magic." Lorenzo dipped a strawberry in some whip cream and placed it in Chantal's mouth. Lorenzo was doing his best to fight it, but he was beginning to fall in love with her too.

"Our sex is magical, but it's not just that. You make me feel alive again. My husband used to make me feel that way years ago. It's been so long, I didn't think I would ever feel that way again until you."

"I don't ever want to fall in love again," Lorenzo stated.

"That means you have been in love before. Who was the lucky woman!" Chantal beamed lifting her body up in the bed. "Don't hold back... do tell."

"Her name was Dior. When I first laid eyes on her, I had to have her... just like with you. She also had a man, but she wasn't married like you are."

"So what happened?"

"Eventually she became my woman and I thought we would spend the rest of our lives together, but it wasn't meant to be," Lorenzo said solemnly.

"Why not? What went wrong? You sound like you really love her."

"I did."

"Did... did is past tense. Why did you stop loving her?"

"I never stopped. She died."

"Dior is dead, oh gosh. I wasn't expecting for you to say that. How did she die?"

"Sway Stone."

"The superstar Sway Stone, was that her boyfriend?"

"Yes. He's responsible for her death and he will pay for it with his own life."

"I think it's beautiful that you're seeking

revenge for the woman you loved and lost," Chantal said laying her head on Lorenzo's chest.

"I think I could fall in love with you too," Lorenzo admitted as he caressed Chantal's face.

"I hope so because I need your love. Please don't get upset, but I have to go. I prom..."

Lorenzo put his finger over Chantal's lips. "You don't have to explain," he said not wanting to ruin the moment.

"I do love you," she locked eyes with Lorenzo and said.

"I love you, too." Lorenzo immediately regretted saying those three words, but he had this magnetic chemistry with Chantal that couldn't be denied no matter how hard he tried to fight it. Knowing that made Lorenzo angry. "I have to get up and use the restroom," he said suddenly.

Chantal was dealing with her own demons and when she felt Lorenzo was pulling away from her she couldn't cope. Chantal reached for the only thing that numbed her pain. She pulled out her vial of white candy that she always kept handy. A couple of sniffs was all it took to make everything right.

"Why the fuck are you putting that shit up your nose!" Lorenzo barked, smacking it out of Chantal's hand.

"It's just coke. Calm down." Chantal gave Lorenzo this bewildered stare.

"Just coke... is that what the fuck you just said?" he scoffed ready to choke her up. "Your husband let's you do coke?"

"Yes. I've been doing it for years. I don't understand what the big deal is."

"So you basically a functioning junkie."

"Don't be cruel, Lorenzo."

"I'm not going through this shit again!" he barked gathering Chantal's stuff up.

"What are you doing?" she cried. "Why are you acting like this? Just a minute ago you tell me you love me, now you're throwing me out." Chantal got out the bed and was following Lorenzo around the hotel suite.

"I'm not doing this shit!" he barked even louder, grabbing Chantal by the arms and throwing her down on the bed. "Dior died of a drug overdose. She was a functioning junkie just like you!" he spit. "I refuse to fall for your type again." Lorenzo let go of Chantal's arms and walked away.

"I'm not an addict," Chantal sobbed.

"Dior used to tell me the same thing," Lorenzo said, leaning against the floor to ceiling window looking out at the New York City skyline.

"You don't understand my life. Ever since I can remember I thought marrying a rich and famous man would solve all my problems. I started off as Andre Jackson's baby mother. I did everything I could to get him to marry me, but he chose Tyler Blake, the movie star, and left me at the altar. Then when I met T-Roc and we got married I thought I had finally hit the jackpot. Boy was I wrong."

"You're married to T-Roc?" During their months of having great sex never did they discuss who Chantal was married to, mainly because Lorenzo preferred it that way.

"Yes, and before you, besides my children, my life was empty. If snorting a couple lines of coke every once in a while helps me numb the pain and make me feel alive, is that so bad." Chantal was now standing next to Lorenzo looking out the window too. She needed to be close to him.

Lorenzo placed his hand underneath

Chantal's chin and lifted her face up. She was so beautiful to him and when he gazed deep into her eyes there was still a slight glimmer of sweetness left. "Chantal, I adore you, but I don't want a junkie."

"I can't lose you, Lorenzo. I'll stop doing coke. I swear."

Lorenzo wiped the tears from Chantal's face. "I wanna believe you, I really do."

"I'm telling you the truth. Please don't give up on me, on us," she pleaded.

"Okay, but no more coke, Chantal."

"No more coke. I promise."

She held on to Lorenzo with dear life. He was Chantal's new addiction. She was replacing one drug with another.

Chapter Twelve

Taken

"Mommy, is this really our new house!" Qiana's daughter, Keisha, asked with excitement as she and her brother ran to the front door.

"Yes! This is it. You and Dion go look around inside and tell me what you think," Qiana said smiling.

Qiana's son and daughter wasted no time

running inside to take a look at the new place they would be calling home.

"Beautiful home. I never would've guessed that someone could afford a house like this working the front desk at the Four Seasons Hotel," Robert remarked sarcastically.

"Thanks for dropping the kids off. They'll see you next weekend for your visitation." Qiana turned around to go inside the house not wanting to get into a long and unnecessary conversation with her ex-husband, but he wasn't having it.

"Have you even thought about what this new man of yours does for a living? He has you in this fancy house that even the partners at the law firm I work for can't afford, driving a luxury car, new clothes, jewelry... how can he afford it?"

"Why do you care, Robert? It's none of your business. We're not married anymore."

"I care because you're still the mother of my children."

"Here we go," Qiana huffed, frowning up her face. "It's amazing you care about me being the mother of your children when it's convenient for you. Where was all that concern when you were out there making a baby with another woman?"

"Qiana, I apologized for that. I will always regret having that affair and destroying our marriage. I would do anything to take that back so we could be a family again."

"Well, that's not going to happen. I've moved on with my life."

"With a man who sells drugs for a living."

"You don't know that!" Qiana shouted, becoming defensive.

"He was arrested by the feds."

"Did he have to serve time?" she shot back.

"No. The charges were eventually dropped, but all that means is he had one hell of a lawyer. But he's still a drug dealer and you know it," Robert barked. "This is the man you want to spend the rest of your life with... have around our kids? Being a drug dealer's girlfriend... that isn't who you are, Qiana."

"Who I am is no longer a concern of yours, Robert. Now stay out of my life!" Qiana stated and slammed the front door.

Qiana sat down on the Persian rug in front of the caste stone fireplace. She could hear Keisha and Dion running through the house, ecstatic about their new bedrooms, big backyard, and the pool they would be able to swim in once summer came. Qiana had to pinch herself to believe this was her life. It seemed too good to be true and in some ways, it was.

Although she wouldn't divulge it to her ex-husband, Qiana was well aware of what Genesis did for a living. After they were shot at a few months ago in front of the restaurant, Genesis came clean and told Qiana exactly what business he was involved in. He wanted to give her an opportunity to stay or walk away. Walking away wasn't even a choice for Qiana. She was in love and being without Genesis wasn't an option.

"Mateo, I wanted to give you a heads up that I'll be making my move very soon," Genesis said.

"Are you sure you want to handle this? I told you, Genesis, I can deal with Tony. There's no need for you to get your hands dirty."

"I want to get my hands dirty. This man tried

to kill me, not once but twice. The first time I was with my woman and he could've killed her too." Genesis's jaw was flinching as he became angry just thinking about the shit. "The second time he almost succeeded. But I'm glad he tried again because if he hadn't, I would've never known that he was behind this bullshit. Now that I know, I want the gratification of killing that motherfucker myself."

"I understand your frustration. I knew Tony would not take it well when I severed our business relationship. Never did I think he would go so far as to take out his replacement. As you Americans say, talk about eliminating the competition." Mateo gave a slight chuckle.

"Well, Tony chose the wrong nigga to fuck wit'. No one tries to kill me, or the people that I love, and get away with it. He should've made sure he got it right the first two times now he gon' die."

While Genesis was at Mateo's estate letting him know of his intent to murder the man who tried to take him out, Tony was across town plotting on how he planned on kidnapping Qiana. Genesis had proven to be hard to kill, but that wasn't deterring Tony. He figured it was time to take a different approach. If he couldn't get to the man then the next best thing was to get what was close to his heart.

This time last year Tony Armstrong was on top of the world. He was the unofficial golden child to Mateo and the money was flowing in. Instead of Tony being content with the millions of dollars he was making he schemed on how he could make more. That scheming cost him his most lucrative drug supplier. Once Mateo found out and cut Tony off his business plummeted virtually overnight. His new plug fucked him over when he placed a huge order and the drugs were no good. He continued to take one hit after another. When Tony found out that Genesis was Mateo's new golden child, he thought if he simply got rid of him, he could then make amends with his former boss and all would be lovely again. That had all changed now.

Killing Genesis had now become an afterthought. Trying to take him out had required too much time without any results. With no money coming in, Tony's high maintenance lifestyle had left him broke. He needed to make some quick guaranteed cash and what better way to do that than holding Genesis's lady love hostage for a large ransom. Tony and two of his henchman had been parked across the street of the sprawling French country estate. They watched as Qiana's two children were dropped off by their father and waited for him to leave before making their move.

"Remember, just take the woman, leave the kids behind. The last thing we need is a fuckin' Amber Alert. I wish we had taken her before those kids even got dropped off," Tony spit. He was tempted to wait and take Qiana at another time, but his gut was telling him he needed to move now.

"We understand, man. We won't touch the kids just take the girl," one of the henchman said as the two men got out the van and headed across the street to Qiana's house.

Qiana was in the kitchen preparing dinner for the kids when she heard the doorbell ring. She knew some more furniture was supposed to be coming, but glanced at the clock and thought it was too late for a furniture delivery. When she got to the door, she saw a man with a beautiful bouquet of flowers.

"Omigosh! Genesis must've sent me some flowers," she gushed out loud as she opened the front door. "Hi, I'm assuming these are for me," she said smiling.

"Is your name Qiana Drennen?" the man asked politely even though he already knew the answer.

"That would be me," she replied reaching for the flowers.

"We know." The other henchman stepped from behind the bushes brandishing a gun. "If you scream or don't do exactly what we say, I will kill those cute little kids of yours," he warned.

"Please, don't hurt my children," Qiana

begged. "Pleaaaaase!"

"Mommy, Mommy, it's time to eat!" they heard Keisha call out coming down the stairwell.

"You better handle that before I do." The henchman nodded his head nudging the barrel of his gun into Qiana's stomach. He made sure the door blocked it's view so her daughter couldn't see the gun.

She swallowed hard as the lives of her children flashed across her face. "Keisha, baby, you and your brother go back upstairs and wait for me."

"But I'm hungry, Mommy!"

"I know, but I need you to go upstairs and take your brother with you right now. I have a surprise for the two of you, but I can't show you until you go back upstairs."

"A surprise!" both Keisha and Dion yelled in excitement simultaneously.

"Yes!" Qiana did her best to sound as upbeat as possible. "Now be a good little girl and take your brother upstairs. I'll be there shortly."

"Okay, Mom!" She could hear their tiny footsteps marching back up the stairs. Qiana wanted to break down in tears, but the only thing she could think about was making sure her kids didn't die because she couldn't keep her composure.

"Close the door and let's go!" the man barked at Qiana once he knew the kids were out the way. She glanced back inside the house then closed the door, praying her kids would be safe and she would live another day to see them again.

Chapter Thirteen

Player Gettin' Played

When Supreme woke up, for a minute he thought he was in the wrong hotel room. After using the restroom he noticed a woman with black curly hair was asleep in his bed. It wasn't until he saw a reddish brown colored wig tossed on the floor did he realize it was Vandresse.

"What time is it?" Vandresse mumbled

coming out her drunk-induced sleep.

"About one o'clock," Supreme told her.

"In the afternoon!"

"Yep. I said the same thing when I woke up. I can't believe I slept this late."

"Well, we didn't go to sleep until six o'clock this morning. I don't think I've ever partied that hard in my life," Vandresse moaned holding her head. "This headache is something serious."

"Why don't you order some room service," Supreme suggested. "A good meal might help."

"Hopefully they can bring me some Excedrin, Tylenol, or something to stop this throbbing."

"Didn't nobody tell you to take two bottles of champagne to the head," Supreme joked.

"Riiiiiight! But that expensive ass champagne was good as hell. When we left the studio and you said we were stopping by a party for a minute, I had no idea it was going to be a full blow out. Yo, it was mad celebrities in there. I had no idea the stars partied so hard."

"Nobody in there was partying as hard as you, though."

"Oh gosh! I was partying that hard?! Please tell me I didn't embarrass myself! I can't lie, there are big chunks of the night I completely can't remember."

"Man, you was jumping on tables. Tryna do cartwheels and shit. I had to get my security to pull you down 'cause they was ready to throw you out." Supreme shook his head.

Vandresse had the most mortified look on her face. Supreme couldn't help but to bust out laughing. "I can't believe I played myself like that. I feel like such a fuckin' loser." She put her head down in despair.

"Vandresse, I'm joking." Supreme sat down next to her in the bed and laughed. "Yes, you did OD on the bubbly, but other than that, you just had a good time like the rest of us."

"I hate you!" Vandresse punched Supreme on the shoulder. "You shouldn't play like that!" she said pouting.

"And you shouldn't punch like that. You got a little muscle on you," Supreme said, playfully squeezing her arm.

"Can I ask you a question, but this one is serious so don't play."

"What is it?"

"I woke up naked... did we have sex?"

"Hell no!" Supreme quickly answered.

"Why you say it like that?" Vandresse questioned sounding offended. "You don't find me attractive no more or something."

"When I woke up today, I didn't recognize you and then I saw your hair on the floor." Supreme laughed pointing to Vandresse's wig.

"It started itching while I was asleep so I ripped it off," Vandresse said feeling even more embarrassed as she reached down to pick it up.

"I'm glad it did because I might've never gotten to see just how beautiful you truly are. Why would you wear that wig when your natural hair looks so much better?" Supreme wanted to know.

"I get bored easily. I like to switch things up. I used to fry and dye my hair so much. When I started going to cosmetology school I realized I was abusing my poor strands. Then I discovered wigs and realized I could have the best of both worlds. Take care and protect my own hair, but still have fun with different colors and styles."

"I can dig that. The same way I like to switch up my shoes, clothes, and jewelry."

"Exactly, good analysis."

"It's still nice to see the real you though," Supreme said rubbing his fingers through her hair. "But to answer your other question. The reason I said hell no like that was because I would never have sex with a woman that's too drunk to know what she's doing. That's like rape as far as I'm concerned."

"Come on now, you don't have to rape anybody, Supreme."

"That's my point. So why would I take advantage of a woman who isn't in a coherent state to say yes. When I have sex with a woman, I want her to want it and remember it."

"You're so fuckin' sexy you know that." Vandresse smiled.

"You pretty sexy too. So what you doing for the rest of the day?"

"Spending it with you... that is if you don't mind having me around."

"I don't mind at all. You crazy, sexy, cool... just the type of chick I like. Now order yourself some food. I'ma go in the other room and return some of these phone calls I missed while I was in the bed knocked out wit' you," he said winking. "When I'm done we can figure out what we gon' get into for the rest of the day."

Vandresse watched as Supreme got up and went into the other room in the hotel suite to make his phone calls. When he closed the door Vandresse jumped out the bed and started dancing around butt ass naked. She thought she had died and went to heaven.

Out of all the ballers I bagged never in a million years did I ever think Supreme would be on that list. Could this nigga really be feeling me like that? Could I really end up being his girl? Will I be able to tell people that Supreme is my man? Fuck being the queen of the hood I can be the queen of the hip hop world being right by Supreme's side, Vandresse fantasized.

"Courtney, what are you doing here?" Tanica questioned, startled when he let himself in with a key.

"Where the fuck is Vandresse? I've been

calling her and she ain't answering her phone and ain't nobody been picking up over here neither," he snarled, grazing past Tanica.

"Vandresse left out early this morning. She said she was going to visit her mom," Tanica lied, wanting to get Courtney out of their apartment without any problems.

"Why the fuck she ain't answering her phone though?"

"I don't know. Maybe she went someplace with her mom and left it somewhere on accident. I have no clue. If I speak to her before you do, I will definitely let her know you're looking for her."

Courtney was walking around the apartment and even went into Vandresse's bedroom. She wanted to tell him to get out, but he did pay all the bills in the place so Tanica felt she had to keep her mouth shut until he was done patrolling.

"You tell Vandresse she better call me before I come back and tear this whole motherfuckin' apartment up," Courtney threatened.

While Courtney was stomping around huffing and puffing about to have a temper tantrum, Tanica wanted to ask him about the mystery baby he supposedly had and the one on the way. Instead, she nodded her head not giving Courtney no lip. He was giving her an unstable vibe, like he was on edge and Tanica was not about to push him over it.

Once Courtney finally left, Tanica locked the door, but this time made sure to use the chain too. Her next move was to call Vandresse.

"Hey, girly, I was just about to call you," Vandresse said sounding extra chipper.

"I see you have your phone."

"Of course I have my phone. You know I always keep that within arms reach."

"Then you must've seen Courtney blowing you up," Tanica snapped.

"So, what he called you looking for me?"

"He did one better. He showed up here on some stalker type shit. He said if you don't call him, he's gonna come back and tear the apartment up," Tanica informed her friend.

"He so fuckin' extra. That nigga ain't gon' tear up shit," Vandresse smacked unmoved by his threat.

"Vandresse, I don't know, he seemed mad shaky. I think you need to give him a call. 'Cause

I ain't tryna see his crazy ass over here again today."

"I can't call him right now. Supreme is in the other room and I don't want him to walk in and hear me talking to Courtney."

"Girl, you wit' Supreme... did you spend the night wit' him?"

"Sure did!" Vandresse was about to go into full blown bragging, but then heard her other line beeping. "Ugh, that's Courtney's dumbass now," she hissed.

"Just answer it and tell him you at your mom's crib. That's where I told him you were."

"A'ight hold on," Vandresse said clicking over. "Hey, what's up," she answered casually as if not having a clue Courtney was tracking her down.

"Where the fuck you at and why you ain't been answering yo' motherfuckin' phone!"

"Why are you yelling at me? I'm wit' my mother, calm down," Vandresse said sneaking into the bathroom to make sure Supreme couldn't hear her.

"So why you ain't been answering yo' phone?"

"We went shopping this morning and I

accidentally left my phone at her crib. We just got back. I didn't even know you had been trying to call me."

"Don't fuckin' lie to me!" he barked.

"Ma!" Vandresse pretended to be calling her mother. "Come over here and tell Courtney I left my phone over here when we left out."

"You don't have to put your mother on the phone," Courtney said falling for Vandresse's bluff. "So when you gon' be home?"

"I'm not sure, but I'll call you when I get there."

"You better."

When Vandresse realized Courtney hung up, she clicked back over to Tanica. "That nigga trippin'."

"Told you! Something off wit' him."

"True, I calmed him down though. But let me get off this phone. I need to be spending some quality time wit' Supreme. He gon' be my boo, you wait and see."

"I hope you know what you doing," Tanica said before hanging up, but she doubted Vandresse did.

"You was supposed to be here two hours ago. I just put Kiana down for a nap." LaQuisha stood in the hallway with her mouth poked out.

"I'll come back later on then if not tonight then tomorrow," Courtney said picking up his keys from the table.

"You don't have to leave. She doesn't nap long so she'll be waking up soon," LaQuisha said wanting her baby daddy to stay.

"I'll be back. I have someplace I need to be."

"What, you going to see Vandresse?"

"That ain't none of yo' business."

"That girl is playin' you. While you giving her money and buying her shit, she fuckin' wit' this nigga named Nico Carter."

Courtney was headed toward the door, but stopped in his tracks when LaQuisha said that name. He didn't know him personally, but heard the name plenty of times. "Where the fuck did you hear that shit at?"

"One of my homegirls fuck wit' his friend Ritchie. They all went out to dinner the other night. She said Vandresse was acting like Nico was her man."

LaQuisha had been itching to drop the dirt she had recently got on Vandresse to Courtney. She didn't want to tell him over the phone as LaQuisha wanted the satisfaction of watching him gag when he got the news that the player was being played.

"Yo' friend don't know what the fuck she talkin' 'bout," Courtney scoffed, not wanting to show he was butt hurt over what LaQuisha told him. He'd been feeling something was off with Vandresse for a minute now, but he was so busy doing his own whoring around in the streets, Courtney didn't put much thought into it. But lately she had been missing more and more so he had a strong suspicion that Vandresse was fucking around, but he had no proof until now.

"Fine, don't believe me. But ask yo' lil' girlfriend about Nico and see what the fuck she say. Liars recognize other liars, so you should have no problem peepin' game when she spits it after you confront her." LaQuisha gave Courtney this smug smirk mixed with a devious grin that made him want to smack the shit out of her.

"I'll be back later to see my daughter," Courtney walked away and said before his temper got the best of him and he mopped the floor with LaQuisha's shit starting ass.

"Take your time. I'm sure you have lots to do." LaQuisha was borderline taunting her distraught baby daddy as she waved goodbye to him. She didn't care as long as it got her closer to getting rid of Vandresse and having Courtney to herself.

Chapter Fourteen

I Love You To Death

"I'll be home late tonight. I'm having dinner with some potential investors for a new project I'm developing," T-Roc told Chantal fixing his tie.

"Okay," she said dropping her silk robe to the floor before getting into the shower.

"No grilling me, just okay?" T-Roc raised an eyebrow. "Where's the interrogation and twenty million questions?"

"You said you're having dinner, what else do I need to know." Chantal's I-could-care-less attitude had T-Roc reeling.

"What the fuck is going on with you, Chantal." T-Roc was now gripping his wife's wrist, making it impossible for her to go into the bathroom to take a shower.

"Nothing! Can you please let go of me so I can go take a shower." But T-Roc wouldn't let up. He kept a firm grip on her.

"Something has not been right with you for the last few months, but lately it's gotten worse and I want to know why. I know you're not stupid enough to be having an affair so what is going on?" T-Roc clutched Chantal even tighter.

"You're hurting me."

"The pain is only gonna get worse if you don't answer my question." T-Roc's words were menacing.

"You've been cheating on me since the beginning of our marriage and I've finally accepted there is nothing I can do about it. What's the point of stressing and worrying about something I have no control over?"

"That better be all it is, Chantal. I would hate to have to punish you."

"And here I thought being married to you was punishment enough." Her ominous words were enough to make T-Roc release Chantal from his grasp.

When Chantal got into the bathroom the first thing she wanted to do was reach for her vial of coke. But Lorenzo popped into her mind and she stopped herself. It was a struggle for Chantal. She never considered herself being an addict because she never had to go without doing coke. It was as second nature to her as someone who would smoke a cigarette when they needed a stress reliever. But now that Lorenzo demanded she not use drugs, Chantal came to the realization that her need for coke ran much deeper than she knew.

"One line won't hurt," Chantal convinced herself taking a quick hit. For that moment T-Roc's words didn't haunt her. She didn't feel like less of a woman because her husband had no desire to be in a monogamous relationship with her. Her mind was free and Chantal was able to embrace a false sense of euphoria.

T-Roc was telling Chantal the truth about his dinner meeting with potential investors, but he had dessert waiting for him at his penthouse on Wall Street in the form of Harper. She was anxiously awaiting T-Roc's arrival, but unbeknownst to her, this wasn't just another night of sexual passion, it would be their last night. T-Roc decided that Harper had become a liability and he already found her replacement. But he wanted one last night of pleasure with the unhinged beauty and afterwards he would cut her loose.

"Baby, I've been waiting for this all night," Harper said seductively deep throating T-Roc's rock hard tool in her wet mouth. He closed his eyes relishing on how superb Harper's head skills were.

"Ahh, Harper," T-Roc moaned in pleasure when she brought him to climax. He watched as she swallowed his cum and T-Roc was tempted to keep her in his staple of women. But then he had flashbacks of what went down between her and Angela and knew he needed to let Harper go. So instead of sliding inside of her so they could have intense and incredible sex one last time he opted to put an end to things now.

"Why are you getting up? I thought we were just getting started." Harper attempted to drape her naked body on T-Roc, but he pushed her away. "Did I not satisfy you? You normally love how I suck you off."

T-Roc felt himself getting aroused again staring at Harper's full luscious lips, the luminous skin on her lithe yet curvy body. But he fought off the urge to bend Harper over the chair and pound deeply inside her.

"This isn't working."

What T-Roc said seemed to come out of nowhere so Harper thought she heard him incorrectly. "What did you say?" she questioned.

"We've had some good times, but this relationship isn't working for me. I think it's time we ended things."

"T-Roc, what are you talking about? We're good together why would you want to end things.

I love you."

"Things have gotten a little too intense and after you attacked Angela it—"

"But I thought we had gotten past that!" Harper shouted cutting T-Roc off. "You said you had forgiven me."

"I do forgive you, but I can't take a chance that you might explode again. Not only am I married, but I'm also a very high profile businessman."

"I promise you, I'll never do anything like that again. I love you so much and seeing that woman all over you made me crazy and I lost it. I'll do better next time." Harper was now holding onto T-Roc. "But you can't end things between us. We belong together."

Harper locked eyes with T-Roc and wouldn't turn away. He could see the desperation in her gaze. "You're a sweet, beautiful girl, but it's over." T-Roc then freed his arm from her hand and did what he does best... write checks. "Take this."

"You're paying me off." Harper's voice cracked, devastated by how cold and unattached T-Roc was being towards her.

"I'm not paying you off. I'm paying you to leave with some dignity."

"I can't believe I thought I was different then all the rest. I thought you loved me too and we would spend the rest of our lives together."

"Harper, I'm a married man. How can I possibly spend the rest of my life with you when I have a wife?"

"But she doesn't make you happy. I'm the only woman that knows how to make you happy," she cried.

"This is the reason our relationship has to end. You want something from me that I can't give you."

"All I want is your love." Harper sounded defeated.

"Like I said, you want something I can't give you," his tone was dismissive. "I'm going to take a shower. When I get out, please be gone, Harper. I'll tell my driver to take you wherever you wanna go."

Harper looked down at the check T-Roc had given her. It was more than enough money to help any woman get over the pain of getting dumped by a married man. But for Harper the check represented being rejected and tossed out of the man's life that she adored, like a piece of trash. Harper refused to accept that fate.

T-Roc was relaxing as he let the twelve shower heads custom designed to cover six zones of your body rain down on him. It came with a computerized control panel to make your shower experience relieve excess stress and bring tranquility. Between the lucrative business deals he closed on a frequent basis, juggling multiple women, and a wife who had a way of getting under his skin unlike any other woman he had ever known, T-Roc needed to invest in as many stress relievers as possible.

He made sure to extend his shower to give Harper plenty of time to be dressed and gone when he got out. T-Roc was feeling so rejuvenated, he was even considering calling over Olivia, the woman he recently met to replace Harper. He exited out the bathroom into his master suite to retrieve his cell phone. T-Roc initially thought he was alone, but when he turned around he realized that wasn't the case. T-Roc grabbed his phone and then rushed over to Harper.

"Hello," a sluggish voice answered.

"Tracy, wake up!" T-Roc barked.

"What is it?"

"I need you to call in my cleanup crew."

That woke T-Roc's personal assistant, Tracy Taylor, right up. "You need the cleanup crew for who?"

"Harper. She slit her wrist. She's lying on my bed dead."

"I was thinking we could take a trip to a private island, go out the country, or just spend a few days in another city far from here. I want us to get out this hotel room," Lorenzo said to Chantal as they ate the food they ordered from room service.

"You're sick of being stuck in this hotel room with me already?" Chantal smirked going through her purse to get her hand wipes.

"I could never get tired of being stuck in a hotel room with you. But I want us to have the freedom to do other things together. Have dinner at a restaurant, go see a movie, or something as simple as going for a walk. With you being married to T-Roc, I know that's impossible for us to do in New York."

"I would love for us to go out of town together. I can tell T-Roc I'm going on a spa retreat for a few days. I've gone in the past so he would believe me. When did you want us to go?" Chantal asked.

"Maybe in a couple of weeks. Is that too soon?"

"Nope. I think that sounds perfect." Chantal leaned over and kissed Lorenzo on the lips before going to the restroom. "I can't wait for us to get away from here." She smiled closing the bathroom door.

He tried to fight it, but Lorenzo found himself falling deeper in love with Chantal. He even began contemplating how to convince Chantal to file for divorce. He no longer wanted to share her. He wanted to have her all to himself. As all these thoughts scattered through his mind, they were interrupted when the phone started ringing.

"Damn!" he muttered out loud when he knocked Chantal's purse off the table while reaching over to answer the phone. After answering the call, Lorenzo knelt down to pick up everything that was on the floor.

"Babe, what are you doing down there," Chantal asked giggling after coming out the bathroom and seeing him on the floor.

"I accidentally knocked your purse over when I was answering the phone. The concierge wanted to make sure we enjoyed our lunch."

"I hope you told them it was excellent." Chantal smiled nervously. "Get up. I can get that." She got down on her knees and started picking up the items off the floor.

"Looking for this?" Lorenzo held up a vial of coke. His face was stone cold.

"That's old. I must've forgot and left it in there," Chantal stuttered and said.

"Don't fuckin' lie to me, Chantal. This shit ain't old," he barked tossing it across the room. Chantal's eyes darted in the direction of the vial. Her first instance was to chase after the coke, but the rage in Lorenzo's eyes made her be still.

"I'm not lying," she mumbled, still on the floor gazing up at Lorenzo who had the scariest expression on his face. "Why are you looking at me like that?"

"Because I can't believe I was actually

considering building a life with you. Asking you to leave your husband so we could be together for real, instead of just hooking up in a hotel room a few days a week."

"I want that too." Chantal began to feel like she was going to hyperventilate. Her eyes watered up.

"Save your tears, they're worthless to me."

"Lorenzo, don't say that. Okay, I did slip up," she admitted. "Stopping wasn't as easy as I thought it would be but—"

"That's because you're a fuckin' addict," he scoffed, cutting Chantal off. "I knew you were, but I wanted to believe you so bad when you said you could stop like that." He snapped his finger. "I heard all those same lies with Dior," Lorenzo said shaking his head in frustration. "I can't believe I fell for this bullshit again."

"Baby, we can get through this. It may take some time, but eventually I will be able to stop. We can do it together." Chantal was now standing up trying to plead her case to Lorenzo.

"The same way Dior had this twisted sick relationship with Sway that kept her going back to him every time shit was difficult, you have that same dysfunctional attachment to your husband. You already told me he has no problem with you doing coke. You'll never stop using while you're married to him."

"Don't you think I know my marriage is built on one dysfunction after another. Doing coke and poppin' pills does make it easier for me to cope, but I'm willing to try because I can't lose you, Lorenzo."

"It's too late, I've checked out."

"You don't mean that. I'm in love with you and I know you're in love with me too."

"Maybe I am, but I don't want you. That high you chasing will always come before me. I already have to share you with another man, I'm not about to share you wit' that white powder too."

"Lorenzo, I'm begging you, please don't do this! I can't imagine my life without you in it. I need you," Chantal wailed.

"That might be true, but you've shown me you need that nose candy even more." Lorenzo grabbed his coat, keys, and wallet and headed to the door.

"Where are you going?" Chantal was

panicking looking for something she could throw over her naked body to chase after Lorenzo.

"I'm going for a walk. I don't wanna be around you while you're getting yourself together to leave."

"Baby, I don't wanna leave. I need to stay so we can work this out."

"There is nothing to work out. It's over for good this time, Chantal. You're married to the right man and you need to go home to him 'cause you ain't welcome here anymore."

Chantal hollered out in anguish when Lorenzo slammed the door behind him and left her to cry her heart out all alone. She glanced around the hotel room they had made love in so many times. All of the memories they shared were right here in this room and Chantal didn't want to leave it. The heartache was becoming more than what Chantal could bear so she did what came naturally. She got down on her hands and knees searching for her medicine. Once she snorted a couple lines of coke all would be better again... at least for the moment.

Chapter Fifteen

Now Or Never

Genesis was leaving Mateo's house when he got a phone call from a number he didn't recognize. He was hesitant to pick up, but decided to. "What's up," he answered.

"Genesis."

"Qiana, why you sound like that and what phone are you calling me from? I almost didn't answer."

"I'm calling you from someone else's phone."

"Are you crying?" Genesis pulled over into a gas station because he could tell something was wrong. "What is going on with you, Qiana... talk to me!"

"I need for you to talk to someone and do exactly what they tell you to do and Genesis please go home and check on Dion and Keisha!" she yelled out before the phone was ripped out of her hand.

"Mr. Taylor, we have some business to discuss."

"Who the fuck is this and why do you have Qiana?!" Genesis pounded his fist down on the steering wheel trying to contain the anger that was bubbling inside of him.

"You're a smart man, Genesis, you know the answer to both those questions if you take a moment and think about it."

"Tell me how much you want so we can get this bullshit over with and I can get Qiana back," Genesis spit well aware that this was nothing but a shakedown.

"I'll be in touch shortly with the amount and

the location of where to bring the money so make sure you answer you phone."

"I'ma kill you," Genesis mouthed out loud when the caller hung up. He then remembered what Qiana said about her kids and sped home. Guilt quickly set in as he knew the lifestyle he chose to live was the reason Qiana had been taken and her kids were now without their mother. Genesis wanted to call out to God, but felt unworthy to do so, so instead of praying he began plotting on her how to murder his enemy.

When Genesis arrived to the house on the quiet cul-de-sac he jumped out of his car and rushed inside. "Keisha... Dion!" he called out hoping the kids were safe.

"Genesis, is that you?!" he heard Keisha say before running down the hallway and standing at the top of the stairwell.

He had never been so relieved to see somebody in his life. "Where is Dion... is he okay... are you okay?"

"Yes, we're fine. Dion is in the bedroom watching television," Keisha said. "Where's Mommy? She was here and then she just left."

"Your mom had to go take care of something,

but she'll be back soon." Genesis went up the stairs and sat Keisha down. "Did you see anything before your mother left?" he asked hoping to get some helpful information without letting the little girl know that her mother's life was in danger.

"She was at the door talking to someone, but I couldn't their face. They brought her some flowers. You see them... they're right there!" Keisha pointed to a bouquet of flowers that had been placed on top of the stand by the door. Genesis turned and saw the flowers. He knew they must've been used to get Qiana to open the door. "Is Mommy okay? Whoever was here didn't do anything to her did they?"

"No. Your mother is fine. Go back upstairs with Dion."

"Genesis, we're hungry. Mommy was making us dinner and then she just left without feeding us."

"She didn't mean to do that. It's my fault. I told her I was going to bring home your favorite."

"You brought us pizza?!" Keisha's eyes widened with excitement.

"I'm going to place a delivery order right now," Genesis said.

"Yippee! Dion, we're having pizza for dinner!" Keisha ran to her brother and told him full of excitement.

Fuck! What should I do with Keisha and Dion while I figure out how to get Qiana back? If I call her mother then she'll grill me about her daughter and if I call their father he'll do the same. But I can't bring them with me because I'll be putting their lives in danger too which isn't an option, Genesis thought as he wrestled with what was in their best interest.

"Hi, Mrs. Johnson, this is Genesis," he said deciding that calling Qiana's mother was the best choice.

"Genesis, hello. This is a pleasant surprise. Is everything okay?"

"Everything is good, but something came up with Qiana and she needed me to watch the kids. But now something has come up on my end so I was hoping that I could drop the kids off at your house for a few hours."

"Of course! My grandkids are always welcome. Qiana knows that. Are you sure everything's okay?" Mrs. Johnson asked with concern.

"Yes, everything is fine. I appreciate you coming through, especially with me asking at the last minute. I'll drop them off in about an hour."

"No problem, I'll be here. See you all soon!"

After Genesis hung up with Mrs. Johnson he then ordered the pizza. He hoped that by the time it was delivered, he would've heard back from Qiana's abductor. In the meantime, Genesis was coming up with his own strategic plan so he could make a pre-emptive move.

After Genesis had dropped the kids off at their grandmother's house there was still no word from whoever was responsible for kidnapping Qiana. He had been racking his brain trying to figure out who had taken her and he kept coming back to one person.

"Genesis, I wasn't expecting to see you back so soon," Mateo said letting him in. "Is there something wrong with the product?"

"I'm not here about that sort of business."

"Then what is it? You seem upset." Mateo noticed Genesis's normal cool, calm, and collected demeanor appeared to be rattled.

"I hate to bring my personal problems to you, but waiting and trying to handle this myself might be the difference between someone I love living or dying. I believe Tony has taken my woman."

"Taken as in kidnapped?" Mateo questioned becoming alarmed.

"Yes. Less than an hour after I left here I got a call from a number I didn't recognize. Qiana told me I needed to do whatever these people said. Then this man got on the phone and he said that if I wanted to get Qiana back I would have to pay."

"How much?"

"I don't know yet. I'm still waiting to hear back, but I'm positive it has to be Tony. Who else out here in these streets would be coming at me like this. My business in Atlanta is low key. I'm telling you it's him."

"You might be right, but let's be sure. Do you have the number you got the call from?"

"I do, but I'm sure it was from a burner or

some shit," Genesis said to Mateo.

"It doesn't matter. I have some people that only require a number to get a location on anyone I need them to. What's the number?"

Genesis pulled out his cell and looked through his call history to retrieve the number and read it off to Mateo.

"Give me a few minutes to make this call. I'll be back shortly."

Genesis watched Mateo go to a back room and he sat down regretting he ever let Qiana into his world. He was tormented thinking how afraid she must be at this very moment and it was eating him up. Genesis preferred not to come to Mateo with his personal drama, but he was willing to set aside his pride if it meant saving Qiana's life.

"My men are ready to move. You just say the word," Mateo came from the backroom and said confidently.

"You have a location?"

"Yes."

"How did you find out so fast?" Genesis was astounded.

"Genesis, I guess you still don't have a full understanding of how far my reach is. I come from one of the most influential families in Mexico. There's not much I can't get done."

"Mateo, I will forever be grateful to you. Thank you."

"Don't thank me yet. Let's first get back your lady love. But if anything, I owe you an apology."

"You haven't done anything for me."

"I should've killed Tony when he betrayed me. If I had he never would've been alive to do this to you."

"So I was right… Tony is behind this." Genesis nodded, needing validation.

"Unfortunately, yes. Tony has reached even lower than I thought possible. But all that will end tonight. So are you ready for my men to make their move?"

"Yes, but I want to be there. I need to know if Qiana is still alive. I owe that to her kids and her mother," Genesis stated.

"I understand. Come, I'll have my driver take us."

Genesis and Mateo arrived in their vehicle shortly after Mateo's security detail had surrounded the location. The three short blocks housed several warehouses, but there was only one that had a van parked out front. Genesis refused to admit it out loud, but he was concerned there was a chance Qiana might not be alive. He found it odd Tony hadn't called back naming his price. He began to wonder had something went wrong and he killed Qiana or if Tony was purposely trying to fuck with his head so that fear would consume him and whatever dollar amount he named Genesis would pay.

"My men are about to make their move," Mateo informed Genesis after receiving a confirmation text.

"Should I be concerned?"

"When guns are involved, you always have to be concerned." Mateo wanted to be honest. "My men know their number one priority is for the woman to be brought to us alive, but there are no guarantees, Genesis."

"I understand. No disrespect, Mateo, I can't sit in this car and do nothing. If Qiana doesn't survive this, it won't be because I didn't do everything I could to save her," Genesis said taking out his gun.

"I respect your decision. Here, take this." Mateo handed Genesis another gun he had on him.

"Thank you. I appreciate everything you've done for me. Now let me go do my part," Genesis said exiting the car. He rushed towards the warehouse, but before he was able to get any closer there was a huge explosion. Genesis's body was lifted off the ground and thrown across the parking lot hitting the ground back first. He struggled to get up as the pain was ripping through every inch of his body.

When Genesis was finally able to rise up and saw all the damage the explosion caused, dread swept over him as he yelled out Qiana's name.

Chapter Sixteen

All The Ways Love Can Feel

"Thanks so much for coming by and bringing some of my stuff," Vandresse said to Tanica when they sat down in the hotel lobby.

"No problem." Tanica handed Vandresse the overnight bag she brought her. "So how long do you plan on staying away from the apartment?"

"It's been nice dodging Courtney for the last couple days. I've decided I want to make it permanent."

"Really? Is that a smart decision under the circumstances? You're not exactly rolling in money. How do you plan on paying your bills?"

"I haven't figured it all out, but I have some money saved. Enough to hold me over for a couple months."

"Get outta here?! I always thought you spent it as quick as you got it."

"I'm not stupid, Tanica. I know you always supposed to save a lil' something for a rainy day. It's just better to make a man like Courtney think you spending and not saving or he won't give you shit."

"Hmm, I never thought about that, but it makes a lot of sense. Smart move, Vandresse."

"Yeah, but honestly at this point I wouldn't care if I only had two dollars in my pocket, Courtney has to go. Between the cheating, the babies and his controlling attitude I'm over him."

"I'm sure it also doesn't hurt that you've been spending all this time with Supreme in this nice ass hotel," Tanica smacked. "I was hoping you were going to invite me up to the room so I could meet him."

"He's actually sleep that's why I had you meet me down here. He was in the studio all night. He didn't get in until this morning."

"Oh, so how's the sex. Does he fuck as good as he look?" Tanica asked boldly.

"We haven't had sex yet. He hasn't even tried," Vandresse revealed.

"What?! No way!"

"Yeah, I said the same thing. I thought I would be the one trying to play hard to get, so I didn't come off as easy, but he hasn't tried to fuck me once. We've kissed a few times and I can tell he's going to be amazing in bed. Great kissers always know how to lay it down in the bed the best," Vandresse said winking.

"So how long do you think you're gonna stay here with him?"

"Not sure, but spending time with him on some chill type shit is what really made me decide that I don't need Courtney in my life. Supreme is rich and famous. He has everything going for him, but yet he's a mad humble, cool dude. Why waste my time with someone like Courtney when I can be with a man like Supreme," Vandresse reasoned. "But then I also have a lot of love for Nico. He's like the ultimate bad boy, but not disrespectful and immature like Courtney."

"I almost forgot about Nico. Have you been in touch with him?"

"We talked a few times via phone and text. He kept asking to see me, so I lied and told him I had to go out of town with my mom for a few days to visit some family. Can you believe I actually felt bad about lying to him?"

"Sounds like love to me or deep like because I've never known you to feel bad about lying to a man."

"Exactly! I'm so torn. I feel like I'm making all this progress with Supreme so I want to keep the momentum going, but on the flip side I really miss Nico. Maybe I can find a way to have both of them. Supreme can be my husband and Nico can be my man on the side," Vandresse waved her hands together and beamed with excitement.

"Bitch, stop dreaming!" Tanica chuckled bursting whatever fairytales Vandresse might of have.

"You never know! Who would've ever thought that I would be staying at a hotel with Supreme for all these days."

"That's a far stretch from becoming that man's wife. Do you know how many women want to marry Supreme and are scheming on how to make it happen?" Tanica rolled her eyes at her bestie as if.

"The difference is I'm here with him and they're not," Vandresse scoffed.

"I can't dispute that," Tanica said shrugging. "But what we can agree on is Courtney is out the picture. You need to let him know soon so he can keep his ass away from the apartment and you can get back the key."

"True. I'll handle Courtney, but right now let me get back upstairs to Supreme. Can't keep the King of New York waiting," she said smiling.

"Girl, you already sprung and he ain't even fucked you yet. You so corny!" Tanica and Vandresse both busted out laughing.

"I know... I know!" Vandresse continued laughing. "But seriously thanks for coming by, girly. I'll call you later," she said giving Tanica a hug. "Love you!"

"I love you, too!" Tanica waved leaving out of the hotel.

When Vandresse got back to the room, Supreme was up and taking a shower. She was tempted to get naked and get in the shower with him, but figured that would be too bold. *We'll have plenty of time for that,* Vandresse thought to herself going through the bag of stuff Tanica gave her. In the midst of that she saw that Nico sent her a text then Courtney started blowing up her phone.

"Nigga, get a life!" Vandresse shouted at her phone and tossed it down.

"You back," Supreme said coming out the bathroom with only a towel wrapped around his waist. His skin was wet and his abs were sculpted to perfection, Vandresse had no idea his arms were so muscular, she was about to have an orgasm just staring at him.

"Yeah, my roommate, Tanica, dropped off a couple things for me."

"I'm just glad you're back."

"Let me find out you like having me around."

"I do. I like your energy. You always seem upbeat."

"It's easy to be upbeat when I'm waking up next to you in this ten star hotel suite," Vandresse commented glancing around.

"I didn't know there was such a thing as a ten star hotel suite. I like that," Supreme said laughing. "I'm glad you like it. Hopefully you won't mind staying here for a couple days while I'm gone. It would be nice to come back and you still be here."

"You're leaving?" Vandresse couldn't mask her disappointment.

"I have a prior engagement that honestly I forgot I had to do. My label committed me to it months ago and I can't get out of it. I wish you could come with me, but it's strictly a business trip."

"Of course, I understand. I appreciate you even considering taking me."

"Of course I wanna take you. You're mad funny. I don't meet a lot of funny, pretty chicks. So does that mean you'll stay here until I get back?"

"Yes! I'll keep the bed warm until you get back."

"I like that." Supreme pulled Vandresse close and kissed her on the lips.

"We can do a lot more than kiss. Give you something to remember while you're gone," Vandresse said coyly.

"I can't. My driver's downstairs waiting for me. I have to get to the airport. But when I get back, I'ma show you the time of your life. I'm talkin' about a helicopter ride, wining and dining, and throw in some shopping. Don't all women love to go shopping... I know my mother does." Supreme smiled.

"Wow, that sounds like the best date ever! Hurry up and get yo' ass back so you can show a girl how it's really done. Clearly the dudes I've been dealing wit' got it all wrong," Vandresse joked.

"No worries... you dealin' wit' an official nigga now. I got you!" Supreme kissed Vandresse on her forehead before heading off to get dressed.

Vandresse fell back on the bed with stars in her eyes. She was celebrating her good fortune. She might've joked about it with Tanica, but Vandresse really was having visions of her walking down the aisle and becoming the wife of rap icon Supreme.

Although Vandresse had dreams of becoming the wife of Supreme aka Mrs. Xavier Mills, she was also itching to spend some quality time with Nico. A girl had needs and since Supreme was playing hard to get with the goods, Vandresse knew that Nico was a sure bet to blow her mind in bed. So she decided to take advantage of the fact Supreme had to go away for a few days and utilize her free time.

"Damn, I missed you," Nico said when he picked Vandresse up.

"I missed you, too." She leaned over and gave Nico some tongue action.

"Yo' people must be making that bread 'cause this a nice hotel they staying at," Nico remarked.

Vandresse lied and told Nico she was staying with some family visiting from out of town.

"Yeah, my aunt owns several beauty salons down south. She's even considering getting one in Harlem. Maybe I can work there after I get my cosmetology license," Vandresse added trying to keep the lie sounding authentic.

"That's dope. How is school coming?"

"Great! I'll have all my hours completed by the end of next month. Then I just have to take the state test. Yeah!!" Vandresse cheered.

"Proud of you, baby. We'll have to celebrate," Nico said caressing Vandresse's thigh.

"You're so sweet! Let me get that license first then we can do all the celebrating we want."

"You'll get your license and then you can have your own beauty salon. Maybe I'll buy it for you as a birthday gift."

"You would do that for me?"

"If you act right," Nico smirked.

"What you mean by that?"

"I thought you was supposed to be gettin' rid of that Courtney nigga."

"I did, I mean I am."

"Which one is it?" Nico pressed.

"I'm done wit' Courtney. I want better for myself. Someone like you."

"Does he know this?"

"I haven't come out and told him yet, but he's

not stupid. I've been avoiding him, not answering his calls. He knows something is up. I plan on letting him know very soon."

"What you waitin' on?" Nico wanted to know.

"You," Vandresse turned towards Nico and said.

"I don't know why you waitin' on me for. I already told you I want you to be my girl."

"I wanted to make sure that was still the case. You know how indecisive niggas can be," Vandresse said laughing.

"Yo, I love yo' silly ass," Nico joined in and laughed too.

"And I love you too, Nico Carter."

That night after dinner, they went back to Nico's place and had the best sex ever. Vandresse felt like they had made love for the first time instead of just fucking. Part of Vandresse wanted to fall asleep in Nico's arms and lay beside him all night, but she knew she couldn't do that. If Supreme decided to call the room in the middle of the night and check up on her, Vandresse wanted to make sure she was there. As much as she was digging Nico, she was not about to fuck things up with Supreme, which meant she had to go.

"Baby, I hate to leave, but remember I told you I promised my aunt that I would be back tonight so I could go with her to Philly in the morning."

"That's right. I forgot all about that. Your body feels so good and warm I probably forgot on purpose. I hate for you to leave."

"I hate to leave too. I can call a taxi so you don't have to get up."

"Stop talkin' crazy! I'll take you back to your hotel. I ain't gon' let my girl take no taxi."

"So, I'm yo' girl now?"

"You tell me."

"Yes, I'm Nico Carter's girl." Vandresse smiled sweetly. "Now give me those lips so I can kiss my man." She tugged Nico's chin and wiggled the tip of her nose against his before they shared a passionate kiss. *Maybe my dream will come true after all. Supreme will be my husband and Nico will be my man,* Vandresse fantasized to herself.

Nico put his car in park when they arrived at the hotel. "You better call me when you get back from Philly."

"I'ma call you while I'm in Philly. Now that it's confirmed you my man, I gotta check up on and make sure you being a good boy."

"Is that right."

"You better believe it. You mine and I ain't tryna share you wit' nobody," Vandresse said.

"Ditto."

"I'll call you tomorrow. Bye, babe." Vandresse kissed Nico goodbye and headed towards the hotel entrance.

"You trifling no good bitch! I knew yo' ass was nothing but a whore," Courtney barked, startling Vandresse.

"What the fuck are you doing here... and how did you find me?"

"I've been following yo' scandalous ass. You

been fuckin' wit' that nigga Nico behind my back. You tried to play me!" Courtney roared, shoving his finger in Vandresse's direction. She had never seen Courtney so upset, but she was so over him, Vandresse didn't give a fuck.

"Yo, get yo' fuckin' ass away from me!" Vandresse popped back shoving her finger right back towards Courtney. "You calling me trifling, but yo' ass got a baby and another one on the way! Go home and change some diapers 'cause I'm done wit' yo' dumb ass. This relationship over," Vandresse stated before turning to head inside the hotel.

"Who the fuck do you think you talkin' to? Bitch, I made you," Courtney shouted, snatching Vandresse's arm.

"Get the fuck off of me!" Vandresse swung back her other arm and smacked the shit out of Courtney.

Nico was still parked in front of the hotel. At first he didn't hear any of the commotion going on because his music was turned up loud and he was responding to a text message that he had just gotten. It wasn't until he glanced in his rearview mirror that he saw Vandresse standing outside talking to someone, but he couldn't see who.

"Who the fuck is she talkin' to? I thought you were already inside the hotel," Nico said talking to himself out loud, confused by what he was seeing. A few seconds later when he saw a man grab Vandresse's arm he quickly jumped out the car. "Who the fuck you think you grabbin' on! Get yo' motherfuckin' hands off her!"

Vandresse and Courtney both turned and looked at Nico, but no one could've anticipated what would happen next. Suddenly without warning, Courtney reached in his back pocket and grabbed his gun. Nico caught it first.

"Vandresse, move out the fuckin' way!" Nico shouted running towards them. He was cussing himself out for not having his gun on him.

By the time Nico's words registered with Vandresse, she was catching a bullet to the head. "You betray me... you die!" Courtney then spit on Vandresse as her blood splattered all over the hotel's revolving door and her body hit the cement. Courtney took off on foot before Nico even had a chance to reach her.

"Baby, no!" Nico hit the pavement and cradled Vandresse's dead body. Part of her face had been blown off. People were now coming out the hotel, some screaming out in horror at the sight of the brain matter splattered on the ground. "I'm so so so sorry, baby," Nico kept saying over and over again feeling numb that he witnessed his woman dying right before his eyes and wasn't able to do a damn thing about it.

The next day when Tanica got word that her best friend had been killed she thought it had to be some sort of bad joke. When it finally set in that it was true, she thought about the last time she saw Vandresse in the lobby of the same hotel she was killed in front of. They hugged and she said she loved her and Tanica told Vandresse she loved her too. Those were the last words they said to each other, which brought Tanica a tad bit of peace from such a horrible tragedy.

"Turn that up." Supreme told an engineer that was in the studio lounge with him. His mouth dropped when they were showing a news clip of yellow tape in front of the hotel he had been staying at for an extended period of time. Then his heart felt like it stopped when a photo of Vandresse came across the screen. They were reporting it was a murder suicide, an enraged man killing his girlfriend. After Courtney murdered Vandresse and ran away, the next morning his dead body was found in his car from a self-inflicted shot to the head.

"Supreme, did you know that girl?" the engineer asked.

"I thought I did, but I guess I was wrong." Supreme then walked over to the television and turned it off.

Chapter Seventeen

United

"You've been in bed for over a week. What the hell is wrong with you?" T-Roc was tired of seeing his wife lying around looking like shit.

"I told you I wasn't feeling well," Chantal mumbled tossing around under the sheets.

"Maybe it's time you go to the doctor, 'cause this shit ain't cutting it." T-Roc reached for his cell phone.

"What are you doing?" Chantal questioned.

"Calling your doctor so I can find out what the fuck is wrong wit' you."

"Hang up the phone!" Chantal demanded.

"Not until you get out that bed."

"Fine! I'll get out the bed," she said flinging the covers off her body.

"I'm still calling your doctor and I want you to go see him today. Do you understand?"

"Yes, I understand. Now can you please get the fuck out of my face!" Chantal screamed.

"Why do I even bother with you," T-Roc complained.

"Because your life isn't complete unless you're torturing me," Chantal snapped, dragging herself to the bathroom to take a shower.

"All I know is you better be at that doctor's office today!" T-Roc yelled out then heard the bathroom door slam.

Chantal saw her reflection in the mirror and she couldn't blame T-Roc for demanding she got out the bed. She looked like crap. She barely recognized her own face. It was called having a broken heart. After Lorenzo ended things between them, for weeks and weeks she begged him to take her back. Chantal even promised to check herself into an outpatient rehab program, but Lorenzo wasn't trying to hear it. He made it clear he was done. But she refused to give up. Chantal believed if she was adamant and continued to pursue the man she felt was her soul mate then eventually he would give them another chance.

All that changed when Jessica Vasquez, a woman that worked at the Mandarin hotel and whom Chantal had become cool with, informed her Lorenzo was seeing another woman. At first she refused to believe it, but then Jessica gave her proof in the form of pictures. He was holding hands and kissing Precious, her daughter's best friend's mother. Finding that out sent Chantal in a downward spiral. Any hope she had of winning Lorenzo back was shattered causing her to then fall into a deep depression, refusing to get out of bed.

"Get it together, Chantal," she said, still staring at herself in the mirror. Then the phone started ringing, but she didn't feel like speaking to anyone. "Gosh, who could that be?" She sighed, picking up the bathroom phone. "Hello."

"Mommy, I can't believe this is happening to me," her daughter said, sobbing.

"Justina, what's wrong... why are you crying?!" Hearing her daughter losing it over the phone gave Chantal a reason to stop feeling sorry for herself and snap out of her funk.

"It's Aaliyah!"

"What happened to Aaliyah? Is she okay?"

"She's better than okay!" Justina hissed. Chantal paused for a moment baffled.

"If Aaliyah's okay then why are you crying?"

"She stole my boyfriend! Her and Amir have been seeing each other behind my back!" Justina wept.

"Honey, are you sure. Aaliyah is your best friend. You all are like sisters."

"I'm positive! I heard them talking about it with my own ears. They admitted it to me. They even kissed. I wouldn't be surprised if they've been sleeping with each other too." Justina continued to sob uncontrollably. "How could they do this to me!"

"Justina, I'm so sorry. It's gonna be okay."

"No, it's not. Aaliayah is dating Sway Stone.

Why does she have to have my boyfriend, too? I hate Aaliyah and Amir both!"

"Honey, calm down. Getting upset like this isn't going to help anything. Where are you? I'll come pick you up."

"No! I have to take care of something. I'll call you later."

"Justina!" Chantal called out, but her daughter already hung up.

Hearing her daughter so distraught was that little nudge needed to send Chantal completely over the edge. "First, Precious steals Lorenzo from me and now Aaliyah has stolen Amir from my baby girl. How dare they. They'll pay for this, mother and daughter," Chantal promised as she stood in the mirror talking to herself. She reached in the drawer and retrieved her stash of pills and popped a few. Chantal had now reached a point where her life was about to spin completely out of control.

It was there in the bathroom Chantal began her diabolical plan to prove her love for Lorenzo by killing Sway Stone. Ruining Precious's life by pinning his murder on her beloved daughter and then getting rid of Aaliyah because she would have to rot in jail for Sway's death. In Chantal's crazy, warped mind this was the perfect solution to all of her and Justina's problems.

"Boss, you seem even grumpier than usual, is everything alright with you?" Tracy questioned while her and T-Roc were putting the final touches on a proposal for an upcoming meeting.

"This woman is driving me crazy!" T-Roc grumbled.

"Not women problems again?! Dammit, T-Roc, I thought you finally learned your lesson after the Harper incident. You said you were going to leave these young, crazy, women alone. If a woman committing suicide in your damn bed don't scare you straight, there's no hope for you!" Tracy shook her head completely exasperated with her boss.

"Tracy, I did learn my lesson after what happened to Harper. I'm still not over seeing all that blood flowing from her wrist."

"I warned you, T-Roc. I told you she wasn't right in the head, but you kept pushing. I didn't like Harper, but I never would've wanted her to take her own life. Then we had to bring in the cleanup crew so nothing could lead back to you, but yet you're still at it. When are you gonna learn... what is it gonna take?"

"I'm not at anything. I havn't been fuckin' wit' no other females. I cut them all off."

"Then what woman is driving you crazy?" Tracy questioned.

"The only one I can't cut off... my wife."

"Chantal always drives you crazy. That's nothing new." Tracy shrugged.

"This is a different type of crazy for her. Everyone knows how vain Chantal is. It's actually one of the things I admire about her. But for the last week or so she hasn't gotten out the bed. She let herself look like crap. No gym or nothing."

"Huh! That doesn't sound like Chantal. Is she ill?'

"She has to be. What kind of illnesss? I don't know. But I made her get out the bed today and go see her doctor."

"You must be really worried."

"Of course I am, she's my wife."

"And you love her, don't you?"

"What kind of question is that, Tracy?" T-Roc sulked.

"Sometimes I forget. Your behavior makes that very easy."

"That's a fair statement. I can't lie, I've made some questionable decisions when it comes to my marriage, but I do love my wife. Honestly, I can't imagine being married to any woman other than her crazy ass," T-Roc said affectionately.

"Maybe it's time you let Chantal know that because I don't think she does," Tracy said thinking about the time she saw her in that hotel a few months ago.

"Trust me, Chantal knows how much I love her. With that ego my wife has, she thinks everybody loves her."

"Boss, I know you have an endless roster of women, but obviously you don't know them that well. If you did, then you would be aware that some of the most beautiful women who appear to have the biggest egos, are actually the most insecure."

Tracy said a mouthful and definitely gave T-Roc some food for thought. He began to wonder if he had been taking Chantal for granted and needed to do more to show her that he did, in fact, love her.

Chantal was high on coke, pills, champagne, and anything else she could get her hands on when she made the decision to use the room key Jessica Vasquez gave her to sneak into Sway Stone's hotel suite and shoot him. In her drug haze she also made the worst mistake of her life by accidentally shooting her own daughter. Chantal hadn't left Justina's bedside and she prayed that her self-serving actions wouldn't cost her child her life.

"Chantal, I really think you should go home and get some rest," T-Roc suggested placing his hands on his wife's shoulders.

"Don't touch me!" Chantal snapped.

"What did I do?" T-Roc was taken aback by Chantal's hostility towards him.

"This is all your fault!" Chantal yelled.

"My fault?" T-Roc asked pointing his hand towards his chest. "How is this my fault?"

"If only you had been a better husband and a more attentive father, none of this would've happened. But the only person you care about is yourself. You're such a selfish bastard and now our daughter might die." Chantal stormed out the hospital room leaving T-Roc in a state of dismay.

After several weeks in the hospital, Justina finally made a full recovery and was able to come home. But getting shot changed her and it wasn't for the better.

"Darling, do you need anything? After Hilda finishes cleaning up, I can have her stop by your favorite bakery and get you some of that cake and ice cream you love so much," Chantal said to Justina who was in her bedroom watching a Lifetime movie.

"I'm fine."

"Are you sure?"

"Positive."

"Okay, well let me know if you change your mind."

"Mom!" Justina called out as Chantal was leaving her room.

"Yes," she said, stopping.

"Remember when I was in the hospital being interviewed by the police."

"Of course I remember."

"I told them that Aaliyah was the one who shot me, but I know it wasn't her," Justina stared at her mother and said.

Chantal walked over to the door and closed it. Then went back over to Justina. "So if Aaliyah didn't shoot you then who did?"

"You did, Mother." The monotone voice Justina was speaking in sent chills down Chantal's spine. Her eyes watered up knowing her daughter knew the truth.

"How long have you known?"

"It started coming back to me a week or so

ago. Little flashes here and there until I got a clear vision of your face pulling the trigger."

"Justina, please forgive me." Chantal fell to the floor begging for her daughter's forgiveness. "I never meant to shoot you. I was so out of my mind. I didn't know what I was doing. Then when I realized what I'd done, I panicked." Chantal's face was riddled with torment.

"It's okay, Mother. I know you only did it for me. You wanted Aaliyah to pay for taking Amir away from me. Well, now she can spend the rest of her life in jail for Sway's murder."

"Justina, you did play a big part in why I did what I did, but there's also another reason."

"Tell me."

"I was seeing someone... another man. I had fallen in love with him, but it didn't work out." Chantal still wasn't over losing Lorenzo and became emotional just thinking about him. "I found out he was seeing another woman and that woman was Precious," Chantal disclosed.

"Precious... Aaliyah's mom?"

"Yes. Finding that out sent me into a depression. Then when you called that day telling me about Aaliyah and Amir, I fell apart. Gosh, I regret what I did that night to you. But I had no idea you would even be in that hotel room with Sway."

"I was so upset about Amir and Aaliyah that when Sway invited me to his room I went. I got drunk and was even tempted to have sex with Sway just to get back at Aaliyah and make Amir jealous," she said with defiance.

"Still, I'm your mother. I'm supposed to protect you, but instead I almost ended your life because I was out of my mind on drugs and booze." Chantal held on tightly to Justina's hand as the tears continued to flow. "I'm a horrible mother."

"Mother, I'm alive so stop beating yourself up. Aaliyah is in jail away from Amir, so everything worked out just the way it was supposed to."

Chantal stared at her daughter and concern consumed her. As crazy as she was, Chantal knew it wasn't healthy for Justina to have no issue with Aaliyah rotting in jail for something she didn't do. But on the flipside, Chantal was the poster child for dysfunctional, so she felt she had no room to judge her daughter. During the next several months, instead of Chantal seeking help for her and her daughter, she spiraled even deeper into her drug use. Every day was one continuous high until the truth finally came out and her darkest secrets were revealed.

"Daddy, calm down!" Justina screamed, tired of hearing her father yell at her mother.

"Don't tell me to calm down, Justina, after that stunt your mother pulled in court today."

"It wasn't her fault so leave her alone!" Justina held her mother closely being protective.

"Please tell me you didn't know what your mother had done!" T-Roc belted.

"Of course she didn't know," Chantal spoke up and said before Justina could answer. She didn't want her husband or anyone else to find out that Justina had known the truth months before revealing it while being cross-examined at Aaliyah's murder trial.

"Good," T-Roc scoffed pacing the living room floor. "Figuring out how to get you out of this bullshit is gonna take enough maneuvering. I don't need the stress of having to do it for Justina too."

"Daddy, you have to make this go away," Justina insisted.

"It's not that simple. Your mother killed a man, almost killed you and set up Aaliyah to take the fall. The DA's office is gonna want to put your mother under the jail cell."

"You can't let that happen! I can't lose my mother. She's all I have." Justina's words felt like a stab in T-Roc's heart. His daughter's love and loyalty was to her mother as if he didn't even matter. He felt he had failed her as a father.

"Justina, can you give me and your mother a moment alone, please."

"Not if you're going to try and make her feel worse than she already does," Justina yelled.

T-Roc put his head down, overwhelmed at the fact his household was in such disarray.

"Justina, it's okay. Give me and your father a moment alone."

"Are you sure?" Justina asked not wanting to leave her mother who appeared so fragile to her now.

"Positive. I'll be fine." Chantal hugged her

daughter letting her know everything would be okay.

T-Roc waited until Justina left the room before speaking. "You've put me and our entire family in one hell of a fucked up predicament, Chantal."

"I know and if you want to get a divorce, I won't fight it."

"A divorce. That's what you want... a divorce. So what, you can try and go back to Lorenzo?"

"Lorenzo doesn't want me." The sadness over losing him remained in Chantal's voice.

"So if he would take you back, you would go to him?"

"Yes, in a heartbeat." Hearing that crushed T-Roc. His ego and his heart took a beating.

"You would choose Lorenzo over me, your husband?" T-Roc sounded dumbfounded.

"Oh, like you care. You don't even love me. You've cheated on me and thrown it in my face our entire marriage. I had to snort coke and pop pills to numb the pain from your constant disrespect. Now you wanna act like you care that I'm in love with another man."

"Don't say that!" T-Roc barked and slapped

Chantal across the face. "You're not in love with him, you love me!" he said shaking Chantal violently as if trying to make her get some sense. "And I love you!" he shouted. "I do love you! I always have."

"Then why?" Chantal broke down and asked. "Why do you continuously hurt me? Why do you always make me feel that I'm not good enough or that no one will ever love me?"

"Honestly, I don't know. I don't have the answer to that question. I do know being with Lorenzo isn't what's right for you."

"It doesn't matter. I was already damaged before I even met you. But after all these years of marriage you've ruined me to the point that Lorenzo or no other man will ever want me. Lorenzo was in love with me, too. Do you know why he dumped me because he found out I was a coke addict," Chantal said between her cries. "I wanted to stop for him, but I couldn't. The hold is too strong."

"Chantal, that's the difference between me and Lorenzo, I understand you. I love you in spite of your flaws and we will get through this."

"What are you saying, T-Roc?"

"I'm saying you're my wife. We exchanged for better or worse. We've both seen the worse in each other and now we're going to work towards the better."

"Is that going to be before or after I spend the rest of my life in jail?"

"Chantal, you're not going to jail. I'll get you the best attorney money can buy and a lot of people owe me a lot of favors. I will use every single one of them to guarantee you never spend one day behind bars."

"And what do you want from me?" Chantal knew that everything came at a price when dealing with T-Roc.

"For one, you better stay the hell away from Lorenzo and I want you to check yourself into rehab. Can you do those two things for me?"

"Yes, I can."

"Good because I want my wife back and I'm going to do everything I can to become a better husband."

T-Roc and Chantal held each other in a loving embrace. For the first time in what seemed to be forever, they were united as one, like a husband and wife should be.

Chapter Eighteen

Saints & Sinners

Seeing the warehouse explode in front of his eyes had Genesis ready to lose his mind. Believing he lost another woman he loved due to senseless violence from living the street life was taking a toll on his psyche.

Right when all hope was depleting, Genesis noticed a man coming out of a warehouse behind the one that had exploded. He was dragging someone that appeared to be Qiana. That jolt of hope got Genesis back on his feet as he sprinted in their direction with a gun in each hand.

"Please, let me go!" Qiana pleaded struggling with Tony as he was pulling her towards the van.

"You better come the fuck on before I leave you here to die," Tony threatened, brandishing his gun to remind Qiana he could shoot her at any moment.

While Tony was distracted with the back and forth drama between him and Qiana, Genesis used the opportunity to sneak around and get behind the van. He waited until Tony put Qiana in the back of the van. When he came around to the driver's side and opened the door to get in, Genesis busted off three shots taking Tony out. He grabbed the keys out of Tony's hand and went around to unlock the back door.

Qiana was huddled in the corner doing her best to hide, fearing that whoever fired the gunshots was coming for her next.

"Qiana baby, it's me!"

"Genesis!" She peeped her head out from a blanket she was using to conceal herself.

"Yes, it's me."

"Oh, Genesis!" Qiana held on to him as she thanked God she made it out of the ordeal alive.

"It's okay. Everything is okay now," Genesis said repeatedly, in hopes of calming Qiana's nerves.

"How are Keisha and Dion?"

"The kids are fine. They're at your mother's house. I'm so sorry this happened to you, baby, but let's go home."

"Yes, take me home." Qiana leaned her head on Genesis's shoulder finally feeling safe again after thinking she may never see him or her kids ever again.

After what happened to Qiana, Genesis had them staying at a hotel until he had a state of the art security system put in place at the house. He wanted to make sure nothing like this ever happened to Qiana again.

"I don't know how some people can do that hotel living. I'm so happy to finally be back in our home," Qiana said, taking her shoes off and sitting down on the sofa.

"Yeah, I feel like fifty percent of the time I'm on the road living in a hotel. It's mos def an acquired taste," Genesis conceded.

"One that I'm not cut out for. But I am glad you got this new security system put in. I feel so much safer."

"I'm glad, baby. I feel much better about going out of town knowing this has been put in place."

"Wait, you're leaving?" Qiana sounded as if she was about to panic.

"I do have to step out for a minute, but I'm not leaving to go back out of town until tomorrow."

"Why do you have to go back out of town so soon?"

"I was supposed to go last week, but I didn't wanna leave you. But I have to handle some things."

"Handle what things?"

"Business, Qiana."

"Genesis, why do you need to continue to do

that sort of business? You have made plenty of money. You can invest or open up all sorts of legitimate companies and leave that life behind you."

"Baby, I really have to go. I won't be gone long. Maybe a few hours max. Call me if you need me."

"Genesis, I want us to continue this conversation," Qiana insisted.

"When I get back home we will, okay," he said kissing Qiana then leaving out.

Qiana poured herself a glass of wine while she mused over some potential business options she could run by Genesis. She wanted to be prepared when they finished their discussion. While considering different ideas she heard the security system announce that Robert was pulling into the driveway. She glanced up at the monitor and saw him and the kids getting out the car headed towards the front door.

"There's my two favorite people in the world!" Qiana smiled brightly greeting her kids before they even had a chance to ring the doorbell.

"Mommy! We're so happy to see you." They both hugged their mother tightly before running inside the house.

"Thanks again for keeping the kids for a few extra days," Qiana said to Robert as he handed her some of the kids' belongings.

"Like I told you before, I always have time for our kids. That's never a problem."

"Okay, but umm, I need to go get dinner prepared."

"I noticed all the extra security you have around the house. Is everything okay over here... did something happen?"

Qiana wasn't expecting for Robert to throw that question at her, but she kept her cool. "Me and the kids are home alone a lot so Genesis wanted to make sure the house was secure."

"I see. So it has nothing to do with you being kidnapped a couple weeks ago." Robert threw it out there and Qiana was not ready. "Don't try to deny it, Qiana. Your mother broke down and told me."

"I don't know what my mother told you, but I'm fine, we're fine... everything is good over here."

"I don't want to take Dion and Keisha away from you but..."

"But nothing! Don't you dare try and take my kids away from me!" Qiana thought she was about to jump on Robert and start whooping him for even insinuating he would try and take Dion and Keisha. "These are my kids!" she roared like a wild tiger protecting her cubs.

"Qiana, I think you're a good mother, but I do have concerns about your decision making when it comes to Genesis."

"That ain't none of your business."

"It is my business when your decisions affect our kids. They were here when you were kidnapped. What if these street thugs had taken our kids too or even worse, killed them."

"But that didn't happen."

"But it could've. Or what if you got killed. How was I supposed to explain to our son and daughter that their mother is dead because she chooses to live with a known drug dealer."

"I don't want to hear any more of this," Qiana stated, ready to close the door in her ex-husband's face. She only hesitated because she didn't want to give him more ammunition to follow through on his threat to try and take her kids away.

"The truth hurts doesn't it? You need to

decide what you want to do and if keeping Genesis is worth you losing your kids."

"Goodbye, Robert." Qiana could no longer take it and closed the door, leaning her back against it. She stared up at the chandelier in the foyer wanting to break down and cry, but she remained strong. The kids had just gotten home and this wasn't the time to get overcome by her emotions. Qiana stuck to her plan, headed to the kitchen and prepared dinner. After they ate, the kids took a bath and played a little bit. Then Qiana read them a story before they were knocked out. Shortly after that, to Qiana's relief Genesis was back home.

"I left some dinner in the oven for you," Qiana told Genesis when he came into the bedroom.

"Thanks, but I ate while I was out."

"How did whatever you had to take care of go?"

"It went smoothly. That's always good."

"Glad to hear. So did you have a chance to think about what I said earlier?"

"Said about what?" Genesis was getting undressed like he didn't recall anything she had mentioned.

"About you running a legitimate business instead of selling drugs."

"I can't do that."

"Why? You have more money then you'll ever be able to spend."

"Says who?"

Qiana's eyes widened. "Says me!"

"What I do isn't just about the money. Yes, I want to be able to provide a great life for my family, but it runs so much deeper than that. It's hard for you to understand."

"Well try to make me understand! I'm trying to figure out why you feel the need to put your life, my life, and the life of my kids in danger on a daily basis when it isn't necessary. You said it isn't about the money, so what is it?"

"This is all I know!" Genesis pounded his fist in his hand. I've been married to these streets for so long that a divorce will never be on the table."

"Are you saying you'll always choose the streets over me."

"Yes." Genesis nodded his head leaving no doubt he meant what he said. "I killed my father when I was eleven years old. I was sent to a detention facility and I've been raised by the streets ever since. To ask me to turn my back on them is like asking me to willingly give up a piece of my soul. I'll never voluntarily do that. The streets will have to be ripped away from me and that will only happen in one or two ways, dead or in jail."

"Then we'll find a way to make it work," Qiana said without wavering. "My life is with you so we'll get through it."

"No, we won't because you want a saint, but I'll always be a sinner. You deserve better than me, Qiana, but this is the best you gon' get and it's not enough."

"Genesis, that's not true. You are the best thing that has ever happened to me. I didn't know what love truly felt like until you came into my life."

"My love isn't lasting. There will always be limitations placed on it. The greatest and most powerful love you'll ever have is through those two beautiful kids you and your ex-husband created. It was selfish of me to even bring you into my world. But when I met you and looked into your eyes, I saw everything I needed from a woman so I had to make you mine. Now I have to let you go."

"Genesis no! I can't let you do this." Qiana buried her face in her hands regretting she even let this conversation begin. "Forget everything I said. I just want things to go back to the way they were."

"You and I both know that isn't possible. You, nor your kids, were born into this life. My son was. This is who I am and who he will be raised to be. I owe you an apology, Qiana!"

"Shut up! You don't owe me anything but your love. I knew what I was getting myself into after we were shot at that night. It was my decision to stay. I didn't let you go then and I'm not letting you go now."

"This I know, that's why I have to let you go. The love you have for me will soon turn to hate, then you'll love me again. You'll battle yourself back and forth with those feelings for a very long time. Eventually, I hope you'll learn to forgive me."

Genesis then started putting his clothes back and gathering some of his belongings, as he didn't keep much in the house. "I'm going to have the house put solely in your name. It's paid for and I also have an account set up for you and your kids. You're an exceptional woman, Qiana. Before I met you, I thought my heart had completely closed to the idea of love, but you showed me otherwise and I'll always love you for that."

"Just go," Qiana cried refusing to even look in Genesis's direction. She knew he was leaving her and never coming back. It felt as if he had taken her very last breath and he was now dead to her. "Please leaaaave!" she hollered wanting Genesis gone so she could mourn his death in peace.

Chapter Nineteen

Hostage To Love

The Present...

"Thank you for seeing me," Nico said when Precious opened the door to let him in. "You're looking beautiful as always," he commented, impressed with how the taupe leather mini skirt she was wearing with a sleek cross front choker, rose-colored bodysuit, paired with snake skin pointed heels accentuated all of her best assets.

"Thank you, Nico. I always appreciate the comments."

"I'm sure you do. But I'm still convinced that you made some sort of secret deal with the devil because time has truly stood still when it's come to your aging process. Something about that ain't right." Nico then sat down on the couch and folded his arms.

"No deals with the devil. If I had, it wouldn't have taken so long for Maya to die. But I'm positive you didn't come over here to discuss Maya.

"No I didn't." Nico unbuttoned his suit jacket and leaned back.

"I see you're getting comfortable. That's a good thing. It means you're relaxed."

"I'm always relaxed around you. You're my comfort zone."

"Nico, you..."

"Stop right there," Nico put his hand up. "I'm not here to try and convince you to come back to me."

"Really?"

"Yes, really. I know you're officially back with Supreme. Aaliyah told me. I know you tried to tell me, but I didn't want to hear anything you had to say after our annulment."

"So what's changed?"

"Recently I had been thinking about all the women that had been in my life; some before you, during you, and after you. A few of them loved me and I loved them too, but I've always only been in love with you. It's time for that to change. I've spent the majority of my adult life not allowing myself to even welcome the possibility of falling in love with someone else. That's how much of a hold you had on my heart," Nico confessed.

"Since we're being so transparent, I guess I have to admit the role I played. Truth be told I never wanted another woman to have your heart. I know it was selfish of me especially once I knew for sure that Supreme was the love of my life, but I loved you too. I still do.

"I get that now. You do still love me, but not the same way you love Supreme and I'm okay with that. You've found your soul mate, now it's time for me to find mine."

"Now it all makes sense. I get why you wanted to see me... you want me to let you go."

Nico gave Precious a half smile. They both were reminiscing about the many years they shared together, some beautiful moments and a lot of ugly ones. Through it all one fact remained intact, their bond was undeniable.

"I know it's hard for you to do the right thing sometimes... because of your selfish ways and all," Nico said grinning, "but yes, it's time we let each other go once and for all."

"Wow, I never thought a request like that would be so hard for me." Precious stood up from the chair she was sitting in and sat next to Nico. The two shared one last kiss. It was passionate, sweet, loving, but most importantly final. "Goodbye, Nico."

"Skylar, I'm not trying to upset you, especially with you being so far along in your pregnancy. But Talisa wanted me to ask you if she could come over and speak with you."

"Speak with me about what? Not telling her the truth about you and leaving her on the island? Gosh Genesis, I don't want to rehash that with Talisa right now."

"I get that, but eventually the two of you are going to have to sit down and talk. Talisa is my wife and you're going to be the mother of my child. The three of will have to get along and that means being open to communication," Genesis explained.

"I get that. But right now all I want to focus on is giving birth to a healthy baby girl. My baby can come any day now and I don't want to be stressed thinking about my conversation with your wife."

"Okay, I'll let her know, but think about what I said too. Also, this is *our* baby." Genesis stressed the word our. I will be in our daughter's life full time."

"How does your wife feel about that?"

"Talisa is an amazing woman and any child of mine she will love like it's her own."

"I see. Well, I'm glad you have it all figured out, but umm, you can see yourself out. I need to go lay down."

"Are you okay?"

"I'll be fine. I'm just feeling a little lightheaded," Skylar said before feeling a sharp pain and her legs buckled.

"Skylar, come sit down," Genesis said holding her up.

"Oh gosh!" They both looked down. "I think my water just broke," a stunned Skylar said to Genesis. Then the contradictions kicked in and she howled out in pain. "The baby's coming."

"Now? You think the baby is coming now?!"

"Yes! Call my doctor," Skylar moaned. Tell him I'm going into labor and you're about to bring me in," Skylar mumbled as her eyes kept opening and closing.

"Skylar... Skylar... are you okay?" Genesis was trying to get her to open her eyes, but she seemed to be out of it. Genesis was afraid for Skylar's life and the life of his unborn child.

Instead of calling Skylar's doctor, Genesis dialed 911. "My ex-girlfriend's water broke, she went into labor and then she passed out. Please tell me what I need to do. I don't want her to lose our baby."

Genesis held on to Skylar praying she would open her eyes and be able to deliver their baby girl.

The Legacy

Keep The Family Close...

Raised By Wolves

Chapter One

"Alejo, we've been doing business for many years and my intention is for there to be many more. But I do have some concerns..."

"That's why we're meeting today," Alejo interjected, cutting Allen off. I've made you a very wealthy man. You've made millions and millions of dollars from my family..."

"And you've made that and much more from our family," Clayton snapped, this time being the one to cut Alejo off. "So lets acknowledge this being a mutual beneficial relationship between both of our families."

Alejo cut his eyes at Clayton, feeling disrespected his anger rested upon him. Clayton was the youngest son of Allen Collins but also the most vocal. Alejo then turned towards his eldest son Damacio who sat calmly not saying a word in his father's defense, which further enraged the dictator of the Hernandez family.

An ominous quietness engulfed the room as the Collins family remained seated on one side of the table and the Hernandez family occupied the other.

"I think we can agree that over the years we've created a successful business relationship that works for all parties involved," Kasir spoke up and said, trying to be the voice of reason and peacemaker for what was quickly turning into enemy territory. "No one wants to create new problems. We only want to fix the one we currently have so we can all move forward."

"Kasir, I've always liked you," Alejo said with a half smile. "You've continuously conducted yourself with class and respect. Others can learn a lot from you."

"Others, meaning your crooked ass nephews," Clayton barked not ignoring the jab Alejo was taking at him. He then pointed his finger at Felipe and Hector, making sure that everyone at the table knew exactly who he was speaking of since there was a dozen family members on the Hernandez side of the table.

Chaos quickly erupted within the Hernandez family as the members began having a heated exchange amongst each other. They were speaking Spanish and although Allen nor Clayton understood what was being said, Kasir spoke the language fluently.

"Dad, I think we need to fall back and not let this meeting get any further out of control. Lets table this discussion for a later date," Kasir told his father in a very low tone.

"Fuck that! We ain't tabling shit. As much money as we bring to this fuckin' table and these snakes want to short us. Nah, I ain't having it. That shit ends today," Clayton stated, not backing down.

"You come here and insult me and my family with your outrageous accusations," Alejo stood up and yelled, pushing back the single silver curl that kept falling over his forehead. I will not tolerate such insults from the likes of you. My family does good business. You clearly cannot say the same."

"This is what you call good business," Clayton shot back, placing his iPhone on the center of the table. Then pressing play on the video that was sent to him.

Alejo grabbed the phone from off the table and watched the video intently, scrutinizing every detail. After he was satisfied he then handed it to his son Damacio, who after viewing, passed it around to the other family members at the table.

"What's on that video?" Kasir questioned his brother.

"I want to know the same thing," his father stated.

"Lets just say that not only is those two motherfuckers stealing from us, they stealing from they own fuckin' family too," Clayton huffed, leaning back in his chair, pleased that he had the proof to back up his claims.

"We owe your family an apology," Damacio said, as his father sat back down in his chair with a glaze of defeat in his eyes. It was obvious the old man hated to be wrong and had no intentions of admitting it, so his son had to do it for him.

"Does that mean my concerns will be addressed and handled properly?" Allen Collins questioned.

"Of course. You have my word that this matter will be corrected in the very near future and there is no need for you to worry, as it won't happen again. Please accept my apology on behalf of my entire family," Damacio said, reaching over to shake each of their hand.

"Thank you, Damacio," Allen said giving a firm handshake. "I'll be in touch soon."

"Of course. Business will resume as usual and we look forward to it," Damacio made clear before the men gathered their belongings and began to make their exit.

"Wait!" the Collins men stopped in their tracks and turned towards Alejo who had shouted for them to wait.

"Father, what are you doing?" Damacio asked, confused by his father's sudden outburst.

"There is something that needs to be addressed and no one is leaving this room until it's done," Alejo demanded.

With smooth ease, Clayton rested his arm towards the back of his pants, placing his hand on the Glock 20-10mm auto. Before the meeting, the Collins' men had agreed to have their security team wait outside in the parking lot instead of coming in the building, so it wouldn't be a hostile environment. But that didn't stop Clayton from taking his own precautions. He eyed his brother Kasir who maintained his typical calm demeanor that annoyed the fuck out of Clayton.

"Alejo, what else needs to be said that wasn't already discussed?" Allen asked, showing no signs of distress.

"Please, come take a seat," Alejo said politely. Allen stared at Alejo then turned to his two sons and nodded his head as the three men walk back towards their chairs.

Alejo wasted no time and immediately began his over the top speech. "I was born in Mexico and raised by wolves. I was taught that you kill or be killed. When I rose to power by slaughtering my enemies and my friends, I felt no shame." Alejo stated looking around at everyone sitting at the table. His son Damacio swallowed hard as his adam's apple seemed to be throbbing out of his neck.

"As I got older and had my own family, I decided I didn't want that for my children. I wanted them to understand the importance of loyalty, honor and respect," Alejo said proudly, speaking with his thick Spanish accent, which was heavier than usual. He moved away from his chair and began to pace the floor as his spoke. "Without understanding the meaning of being loyal, honoring and respecting your family, you're worthless. Family forgives but some things are unforgivable so you have no place on this earth or in my family."

Then without warning and before anyone had even noticed, all you saw was blood squirting from Felipe's slit throat. Then with the same precision and quickness, Alejo took his sharp pocketknife and slit Hector's throat too. Everyone was too stunned and taken aback to stutter a word.

Alejo then wiped the blood off his pocket-knife on the white shirt that a now dead Felipe was wearing. He kept wiping until the knife was clean. "That is what happens when you are dis-loyal. It will not be tolerated...ever." Alejo made direct contact with each of his family member at the round table then focused on Allen. "I want to personally apologize to you and your sons. I do not condone what Felipe and Hector did and they have now paid the price with their lives."

"Apology accepted," Allen said.

"Yeah, now lets get the fuck outta here," Clayton whispered to his father as the three men stood in unison not speaking another word until they were out the building.

"What type of shit was that?" Kasir mumbled.

"I told you that old man was fuckin' crazy," Clayton said shaking his head as they got into their waiting SUV.

"I think we all knew he was crazy just not that crazy. Alejo know he could've slit them boys throats after we left," Allen huffed. "He just wanted us to see the fuckin' blood too and ruin our afternoon," he added before chuckling.

"I think it was more than just that," Clayton replied, looking out the tinted window as the driver pulled out the parking lot.

"Then what?" Kasir questioned.

"I think old man Alejo was trying to make a point, not only to his family members but to us too."

"You might be right, Clayton."

"I know I'm right. We need to keep all eyes on Alejo 'cause I don't trust him. He might've killed his crooked ass nephews to show good faith but trust me that man hates to ever be wrong about anything. What he did to those nephews is probably what he really wanted to do to us but he knew nobody would've left that building alive. The only truth Alejo spoke in there was that he was raised by wolves," Clayton scoffed leaning back in the car seat.

All three men remained silent for the duration of the drive. Each pondering what had transpired in what was supposed to be a simple business meeting that turned into a double homicide. They also thought about the point Clayton said Alejo was trying to make. No one wanted that to be true as their business with the Alejo family was a lucrative one for everyone involved. But for men like Alejo, sometimes pride held more value than the almighty dollar, which made him extremely dangerous.

P.O. Box 912
Collierville, TN 38027

www.joydejaking.com
www.twitter.com/joydejaking

A King Production

ORDER FORM

Name:

Address:

City/State:

Zip:

QUANTITY	TITLES	PRICE	TOTAL
	Bitch	$15.00	
	Bitch Reloaded	$15.00	
	The Bitch Is Back	$15.00	
	Queen Bitch	$15.00	
	Last Bitch Standing	$15.00	
	Superstar	$15.00	
	Ride Wit' Me	$12.00	
	Ride Wit' Me Part 2	$15.00	
	Stackin' Paper	$15.00	
	Trife Life To Lavish	$15.00	
	Trife Life To Lavish II	$15.00	
	Stackin' Paper II	$15.00	
	Rich or Famous	$15.00	
	Rich or Famous Part 2	$15.00	
	Rich or Famous Part 3	$15.00	
	Bitch A New Beginning	$15.00	
	Mafia Princess Part 1	$15.00	
	Mafia Princess Part 2	$15.00	
	Mafia Princess Part 3	$15.00	
	Mafia Princess Part 4	$15.00	
	Mafia Princess Part 5	$15.00	
	Boss Bitch	$15.00	
	Baller Bitches Vol. 1	$15.00	
	Baller Bitches Vol. 2	$15.00	
	Baller Bitches Vol. 3	$15.00	
	Bad Bitch	$15.00	
	Still The Baddest Bitch	$15.00	
	Power	$15.00	
	Power Part 2	$15.00	
	Drake	$15.00	
	Drake Part 2	$15.00	
	Female Hustler	$15.00	
	Female Hustler Part 2	$15.00	
	Female Hustler Part 3	$15.00	
	Princess Fever "Birthday Bash"	$9.99	
	Nico Carter The Men Of The Bitch Series	$15.00	
	Bitch The Beginning Of The End	$15.00	
	Supreme...Men Of The Bitch Series	$15.00	
	Bitch The Final Chapter	$15.00	
	Stackin' Paper III	$15.00	
	Men Of The Bitch Series And The Women Who Love Them	$15.00	
	Coke Like The 80s	$15.00	

Shipping/Handling (Via Priority Mail) $6.50 1-2 Books, $8.95 3-4 Books add $1.95 for ea. Additional book.

Total: $_____ FORMS OF ACCEPTED PAYMENTS: Certified or government issued checks and money Orders, all mail in orders take 5-7 Business days to be delivered